Charles W. DeLacy Evans

Can we Prolong Life?

An inquiry into the cause of old age and natural death, showing the diet and agents

best adapted for a lengthened prolongation of existence

Charles W. DeLacy Evans

Can we Prolong Life?
An inquiry into the cause of old age and natural death, showing the diet and agents best adapted for a lengthened prolongation of existence

ISBN/EAN: 9783337387549

Printed in Europe, USA, Canada, Australia, Japan

Cover: Foto ©Andreas Hilbeck / pixelio.de

More available books at **www.hansebooks.com**

CAN WE PROLONG LIFE?

AN INQUIRY INTO THE CAUSE OF "OLD AGE" AND
"NATURAL DEATH," SHOWING THE DIET AND
AGENTS BEST ADAPTED FOR A *LENGTHENED*
PROLONGATION OF EXISTENCE.

BY

CHAS. W. DE LACY EVANS, M.R.C.S.E.

LONDON:

BAILLIÈRE, TINDALL, AND COX,

KING WILLIAM STREET, STRAND.

[PARIS AND MADRID.]

1879.

𝔗𝔥𝔦𝔰 𝔚𝔬𝔯𝔨 𝔦𝔰 𝔇𝔢𝔡𝔦𝔠𝔞𝔱𝔢𝔡

TO THE

MEDICAL AND SURGICAL STAFF

OF

ST. THOMAS'S HOSPITAL;

AS A TOKEN OF REGARD

FOR THE MANY BENEFITS RECEIVED FROM ONE AND ALL

DURING A STUDENT LIFE

AT THE

MEDICAL AND SURGICAL COLLEGE

OF THE ABOVE INSTITUTION.

CHAS. W. DE LACY EVANS.

PREFACE.

In every being throughout animated nature, from the most insignificant insect to the most enlightened, ennobled, and highly-developed human being, we notice a deeply-rooted love for one possession before all others, and that is the possession of *Life*. What will not a man give to preserve his life? What would he not give to prolong it? The value of riches, titles, honour, power and worldly prospects are as nought compared with the value which every sane man, however humble, and even miserable, places on the preservation of his life.

Human life, physically considered, is a chemico-animal operation; and whatever it may be as an abstract principle, the manifestations and phenomena of life are dependent upon matter in a state of change by the united powers of Nature, and are embodied in a few elementary and grand physical and chemical processes.

The laws of life and of death, looked upon in this light, form the basis of a fixed science—the MACRO-BIOTIC, or the art of prolonging life.

There is, however, a distinction to be made between this art and the science of medicine, but the one is auxiliary to the other.

There is a state of body which we term *health; plus* or *minus* divergences from this path we call *disease.* The object of medicine is to guide these variations to a given centre of bodily equilibrium; but the object of the macrobiotic art is by the founding of dietetic and other rules, on general principles, to preserve the body in health, and thereby prolong life.

In the present work the author has attempted to go beyond this, by inquiring into the *causes* which have a share in producing the changes which are observed as age advances, and, further, by pointing out a means of checking them.

" He who writes, or speaks, or meditates, without facts as landmarks to his understanding, is like a mariner cast on the wide ocean, without a compass or a rudder to his ship." If he conceives an idea, a phantom of his own imagination, and attempts to make it a reality by accepting only those facts or phenomena which accord with his premature conception, ignoring those which contradict this shadow or idea, but which may nevertheless be demonstrably true, he creates a *theory,* which may be incorrect, and if so it is doomed, sooner or later, to destruction. Although it possibly required but a few hours to construct, centuries may elapse before it is finally destroyed. The founder of an erroneous hypothesis creates a *monster*, which only serves to combat and stifle *Truth*. The struggle can last for a time only, for Truth must of necessity ultimately prevail.

" The true philosopher always seeks to explain and illustrate nature by means of *facts*, of phenomena; that is, by experiments, the devising and discovery of which is his task, and by which he causes the object of his investigation to speak as it were intelligibly to him; but it is by carefully observing and arranging all such facts as are in connection with it, that insight into its nature is attained. For we must never forget that *every phenomenon has its reason, every effect its cause.*"—BACON.

" The history of science gives us the consoling assurance that we shall succeed, by pursuing the path of experiment and observation, in unveiling the mysteries of organic life, and that we shall be enabled to obtain decided, definite answers to the question—What are *causes* which have a share in producing vital phenomena ?"—LIEBIG.

" Let no man be alarmed at the multitude of the objects presented to his attention; for it is this, on the contrary, which ought rather to awaken hope . . . If there were any one amongst us who, when interrogated respecting the objects of nature, was always prepared to answer by *facts*, the discovery of causes and the foundation of all sciences would be the work of a few years."—BACON.

The purpose of the author in publishing this work is to make known the results of inquiries into the causes of what is termed the " decay of nature," not theoretically or by accepting only those facts which accord with a preconceived idea, but by collecting facts bearing on the subject, and making clear and straightforward deductions therefrom.

It is not written for the purpose of conveying a signification of man's individual greatness, nor of ignoring a Supreme Being. It is our increasing knowledge of the phenomena of nature, and the laws by which they are regulated, which makes us conscious of, and teaches us to recognise, the perfection, the greatness, and unfathomable wisdom of an all-wise CREATOR, whose works and actions become daily more manifest in their illimitable impressions, the sublimity and greatness of which the human mind is not capable of conceiving. The most untiring imagination—the most exalted mind —will contemplate images and fashion forms, which, when compared with reality, appear but as bubbles of brilliant and changing colours—to vanish, leaving the contemplator in forced recognition of his own frailties and imperfections, but not enlightened on the inscrutable wisdom of an infinitely higher Being.

This work is founded upon a paper on " Ossification the Cause of 'Old Age,'" read by the author before the St. Thomas's Hospital Medical and Physical Society, on Oct. 26, 1876.

The author first conceived the idea of the possible prolongation of existence from a publication entitled " Patriarchal Longevity," by " Parallax," and most of the instances of longevity are taken from " Records of Longevity," by Easton and Bailey, and Hufeland's " Art of Prolonging Life," edited by Erasmus Wilson, F.R.S.

It has long been the opinion of scientific men, that by suitable diet and regularity, the blessings of life may be enjoyed in fair health to a " green old age." The purpose of this work is to show that we may for a time curb the *causes* which are visible in *effect* as age advances, and thus prolong life, and further, that by other means, founded upon simple fact, we may accomplish this for a lengthened period.

The author's attempt to deal with a matter of such vast importance as the prolongation of life will necessarily subject him to severe and probably adverse criticism. In the first edition of a book hurriedly written in moments snatched from the turmoil of a general practice, many minor errors are sure to be found; but as the author takes facts for a beacon, there is no error in principle. He will only ask those who criticise to imagine themselves for the time in the position of Astrea, the Goddess of Justice, and not to weigh the evidence with one scale heavily laden with prejudice.

The purpose of the author is to help to benefit man's existence : if he partially accomplishes this object—if in casting, as it were, a widow's mite into the well-stocked coffers of literature, he can claim to have even slightly benefited humanity, the reward he asks will be granted.

CHAS. W. DE LACY EVANS.

44, Fulham Road,
South Kensington.
Feb. 1879.

8 Osnaburg St.
Regents Park

CAN WE PROLONG LIFE?

CHAPTER I.

THE CAUSE OF "OLD AGE" AND "NATURAL DEATH."

WITH all our physiological, anatomical, and philosophical discoveries, there are left many questions at present not solved; amongst others, the action of the brain, thought, motion, life, and the possible prolongation of existence.

"Nature speaks to us in a peculiar language, in the language of phenomena. She answers at all times questions which are put to her; and such questions are experiments."

In "old age" the body differs materially from youth in actions, sensibility, function, and composition. The active, fluid, sensitive, and elastic body of youth, gradually gives place to induration, rigidity, and decrepitude, which terminates in "natural death."

In nature there are distinct reasons for every change,

1

for development, growth, decomposition, and death. If with our minds free from theory, and unbiassed by hypotheses, we ask nature the cause of these changes, she will surely answer us. Let us ask her the cause of these differences between youth and old age. Why the various functions of the body gradually cease? Why we become "old" and die?

The most marked feature in old age is that a fibrinous, gelatinous, and earthy deposit has taken place in the system; the latter being composed chiefly of phosphate and carbonate of lime, with small quantities of sulphate of lime, magnesia, and traces of other earths.

Among physiologists and medical philosophers generally, the idea prevails that the "ossification" (or the gradual accumulation of earthy salts in the system) which characterises "natural death," is the *result* of "old age," but investigation shows that such an explanation is unsatisfactory. For in the first place, if "old age" (which is really the number of years a person has lived) is the cause of the ossification which accompanies it, then, if "like causes produce like effects," *all* of the same age should be found in the same state of ossification, but investigation proves beyond all doubt that such is not the case. How common it is to see individuals about fifty years old, as aged and decrepit as others at seventy or eighty!

We will first inquire into the differences found by investigation between youth and old age, in the many structures and organs of the body.

Bone.—The average constituents of bone at about

the prime of life, according to an analysis by Berzelius, are :

Organic matter, gelatin and bloodvessels	.		33·30
Inorganic or Earthy matter	Phosphate of lime	. .	51·04
	Carbonate of lime	. .	11·30
	Fluoride of calcium	. .	2·00
	Phosphate of magnesia .	.	1·16
	Soda and chloride of sodium .		1·20
			100·00

Thus we see that 66·7 per cent., or about two-thirds, are composed of inorganic or earthy compounds. The organic or gelatinous portion contains about 10 per cent. of water (if recent).

Compact bony substance contains more earthy matter than the spongy bone; and, proportionally, more phosphate of lime to the carbonate than the latter.

If we take the bones of a *child*, of a *young man* in the prime of life, and of an *old man*, and subject a given weight of each of them to a simple analysis, the earthy constituents of which may be easily obtained by subjecting them to a strong heat, with free access of air, by which means the animal or organic matter is entirely consumed, the earthy part remaining, and carefully weigh the residue of earthy salts, what do we find ?

That the bones of the child contain a certain amount of earthy compounds (according to its age) ; that the bones of the young man contain a larger proportion of earthy compounds than those of the child, and that the bones of the old man contain a larger proportion than either. If we also take the stages intermediate between childhood and manhood, on the one hand, and manhood and old age on the other, we obtain the same result, clearly showing that from some cause the amount of earthy compounds in the bones gradually increases from birth to old age.

" According to Schreger and others, there is a considerable increase in the earthy constituents of bones with advancing years. Dr. Rees states that this is especially marked in the long bones and the bones of the head, which, in the foetus, do not contain the excess of earthy matter found in those of the adult. . . . Thus in the child, where the animal matter predominates, it is not uncommon to find, after an injury to the bones, that they become bent, or only partially broken, from the large amount of flexible animal matter which they contain. Again also in aged people, where the bones contain a large proportion of earthy matter, the animal matter at the same time being deficient in quantity and quality, the bones are more brittle, their elasticity is destroyed, and hence fracture takes place more readily."—GRAY.

From embryonic life to birth a gradual process of ossification is going on, and even at birth the epiphyses of most of the cylindrical bones, all the bones of the carpus, the five smaller ones of the tarsus, the patella, sesamoid bones, and the last pieces of the coccyx are still unossified.

From birth this process of ossification still continuing, the epiphyses become united to their shafts, the ossific centres of the vertebræ and cranium gradually join to form their respective bones, and it is not till about the thirtieth year that the full development of the bones of the skeleton is attained. From the prime of life we trace onward this gradual process of ossification ; the inter-vertebral cartilages become shrunken, hard, and inelastic, causing in old age diminished stature and an inclination to bend forwards; in some instances the sutures of the cranium are gradually obliterated, and the once separate bones unite; the cartilages of the ribs, and articular ends of bones harden and ossify; the bones of the sternum unite; from loss of teeth changes are observed in the shape of the lower jaw; the segments of the hyoid bone become united together, forming in old age a single bone ; the cartilages of the larynx become ossified; even the ligaments of joints become so hardened, that their former pliability is usurped by the limited, awkward, and decrepit movements of old age.

Thus we find that the bones at this period of life contain proportionately more earthy matter than those in youth.

Muscles.—As age advances the muscles diminish in bulk, the fibres become rigid and less contractile, becoming paler or even yellowish in colour, and are not influenced by stimuli to the same extent as in youth.

Tendons, and adjacent portions of muscular tissue and aponeuroses become hardened and even ossified. There is also a diminution in the fluid in the sheaths of the tendons.

If we analyse a given weight of muscular tissue taken from an *old* man, and the same weight taken from a *young* man, we find that the former contains more earthy matter than the latter. Any structure or organ of the body will give the same result, *i.e.*, that there exists throughout the system more earthy matter in old age than in adolescence, and that this earthy matter has been gradually accumulating from the first stage of existence.

Brain.—We will next briefly consider the alterations in the brain and nerve centres in old age.

The brain—the organ which presides over every thought and action of our material bodies, which constitutes one of the great central masses of the nervous system, and which is in constant telegraphic communication with every structure and part of the body, through the medium of the spinal column and nerves, the latter of which are so wonderfully distributed by their minute ramifications, that there is not a point on the whole surface of the body, the size of a pin's head, which we could wound, without the brain being at once cognisant of the fact—differs from most other organs and structures of the body in containing phosphorus, in an unoxidised form, upon which subject we will treat hereafter.

The brain grows or increases in size up to about forty years of age, when it reaches its maximum weight. After this period there is a gradual and slow diminution in weight of about one ounce in every ten years.

According to Cazanvieilh, the longitudinal diameter of the brain of an *old man,* compared with that of a *young man,* is six inches one line, French measure, for the former, and six inches four lines for the latter ; whilst the transverse diameter is four inches ten lines in the *old man*, and five inches in the *young man*. The same authority gives the comparative measurements of different parts of the brain at the three periods of life, puberty, prime of life, and old age, as under :

	PERSONS AT PUBERTY.		PRIME OF LIFE.	OLD AGE.
		in. lns.	in. lns.	in. lns.
Thal. optici		1 5½	1 6	1 4½
Corp. striata		2 6	2 6	2 4½
Corp. callosum		3 4½	3 5	2 7
Mesocephalon	{ length	0 10	0 11	0 10½
	{ breadth	1 0	1 1	1 0
Cerebellum	{ length	2 2	2 3	2 3
	{ breadth	3 9	3 9	3 9

Thus it appears that with the exception of the cerebellum (or animal brain), every part of the encephalon diminishes in size in old age. Further, the convolutions of the brain become less and less distinct and prominent.

Membranes of the Brain.—The *dura mater* is often found apparently collapsed or corrugated, particularly in the very aged, when little fluid is found beneath it ; it is frequently found to be thickened and indurated, and ossific deposits on the arachnoid surface are very common. These are generally described as resulting from a chronic inflammatory action, but where during life there have been no symptoms of any inflammatory disease, we must put it down as concomitant to "old age," or that gradual process of ossification which either accompanies or causes such a state of the system.

Thickening and opacity of the *arachnoid* are often found in old people, the fluid secreted being sometimes turbid and albuminous ; the membrane is sometimes found to have an abnormal dryness, and osseous deposits sometimes, though rarely, occur ; but a roughness or grittiness, giving the sensation of fine sand under the finger, is more often met with, this roughness being due to earthy deposits. The choroid plexus is sometimes in a varicose state, and the membranes lining the ventricles are found thick and opaque.

We now come to the most important change of all, which fully accounts for the many differences in the brain existing between youth and old age, that is, the changes in the bloodvessels supplying it. The arteries in old age become thickened and lessened in calibre from fibrinous, gelatinous, and earthy deposits. This is more easily detected in the larger vessels; but all, even to the most minute subdivisions, undergo the same gradual change. Thus the supply of blood to the brain becomes less and less ; hence the diminution in size of the organ from the prime of life to old age ; hence the functions of the brain become gradually impaired ; the vigorous brain of middle life gradually giving place to loss of memory, confusion of ideas, inability to follow a long current of thought, notions oblivious of the past and regardless as to the future, carelessness of momentary impressions, softening of the brain, and that imbecility so characteristic of extreme age.

In the brain, "the arteries most commonly found

ossified are the internal carotids and the basilar; but the circle of Willis, and the vessels departing from it, as well as the arterial ramifications which appear between the convolutions, and come out upon the surface, often participate more or less in this morbid state. Cartilaginous degeneration is still more extensive, and seems to precede the ossific deposits. Cartilaginous and ossific formations in the coats of arteries of the brain occasion irregular distribution of blood, and interrupted or imperfect supplies of this fluid to some parts of the organ, disposing to aneurismal dilatations, to rupture, and consequently to the production of apoplexy and paralysis."—COPLAND.

" *Ossification* is detected (with the naked eye) only in the *arteries;* but it occurs in them very frequently, and to a very great extent, particularly in advanced life."—*Ibid.*

" *After the age of fifty,* the walls of the bloodvessels are very liable to ' degeneration.' The aorta, in particular, becomes dilated, the elasticity of its walls impaired, and its inner surface roughened by large, irregular, whitish, elevated patches of morbid matter, lying immediately beneath a superficial layer of the inner coat, and composed of a mixture of *earthy and fatty matter.* . . . In the *smaller* arteries, the ossification proceeds much more uniformly, and they become at last more or less completely converted into *smooth bony tubes.* The capillaries are equally liable with the arteries to degeneration."—HOOPER'S " Physician's Vade Mecum."

" The cerebral arteries of old persons are frequently found studded with cartilaginous and osseous laminæ."

" The ossification of arteries has been ascribed by many authors to *slight* chronic inflammatory action. The experiments of M. Rayer and M. Cruveilheir seem to confirm this inference, as an *occasional* occurrence at least, particularly in the fibrous and cartilaginous structures, increased vascular action of these structures, artificially excited, being generally followed by ossiform depositions ; but in a number of cases, particularly in those where the deposit takes place in the cellular tissues, *no inflammatory action can be detected* previously to this change ; besides, increased vascular action frequently exists, without being attended with ossiform depositions. This lesion, therefore, cannot be altogether ascribed to this cause, although frequently resulting from it in a certain order of tissues. It would be correct to consider it merely as a consequence of disorder of the *natural* process of nutrition and secretion. . . . But *to what cause* is this disorder of the nutritive function to be imputed, particularly when it occurs in parts which have *not evinced any sign of inflammatory action,* as in the cellular tissue connecting the internal coats of *arteries?* The importance of this inquiry may appear, from the *very great proportion of persons in advanced years* who are affected in some organ or tissue with this lesion, and from the remarkable part it performs in the production of a number of diseases of the most dangerous description."—COPLAND's " Med. Dic.," art. " Arteries."

MM. Rostan, Recamier, and others, agree in considering that softening of the brain is occasionally unconnected with any inflammatory action, *particularly in aged persons.*

We have quoted from the above authorities to show that ossification and thickening of the arteries of the brain has not been overlooked, but that it is a fact which has been known for many years; also to show that this gradual process of ossification is not due to any inflammatory action. And we shall show that this earthy matter has been deposited from the blood, and increases year by year with old age, thus lessening the calibre of the larger vessels, partially, and in some cases fully, "clogging up" the capillaries, gradually diminishing the supply of blood to the brain, causing its diminution in size in old age, and fully accounting for the gradual loss of the mental capabilities before enumerated.

As age advances, the energies of the *ganglial system* decline; digestion, circulation, and the secretory functions are lessened; the *ganglia* diminish in size, become firmer, and of a deeper hue. In old age the *nerves* become tougher and firmer, the medullary substance diminishes, and their bloodvessels lessen in calibre. The sensibility of the whole cerebro-spinal system decreases, hence diminution of the intellectual powers, lessened activity and strength in the organs of locomotion in advanced age.

Another important and striking fact is that the brain of an old man contains a less amount of phosphorus than that of a younger man.

Arteries.—As with the arteries of the brain, the same process of gradual ossification extends to every vessel, the arborescent ramifications of which supply, without exception, every part of the system. Bichat and Baillie considered that the larger proportion of persons above sixty years of age have some part of the arterial system affected by these depositions.

Veins.—In old age the *vasa vasorum* decrease and become indistinct, the arteries lessen in calibre, they therefore hold a less amount of blood than in younger life; the pressure is thrown on the veins, which dilate, their coats becoming thinner, they become tortuous or even varicose.

Heart.—In the heart "the coronary arteries are frequently ossified both in their trunks and in their subdivisions." In many cases this ossification is not visible; but, on analysing the same weight of muscular tissue taken from the heart of two individuals at different stages of life, we find the same excess of earthy matter in old age as we did in other structures already considered; the capillaries gradually diminish in calibre, the muscular fibres of the organ are improperly nourished, the fibres become paler in colour, the cavities dilated and their walls thinned, in some cases becoming more or less hardened or indurated, in others giving way to fatty degeneration. The valves also undergo cartilaginous and osseous transformations. The supply of blood to the organ is gradually diminished, and its feeble contractions impel the blood along vessels already indurated and ossified, to organs which have undergone the same degree of ossification, and are therefore unable to properly perform their necessary functions.

"About the age of forty, and still more so as the age of fifty is approached, the sanguineous circulation becomes more and more languid, particularly in the veins; hence the frequency of venous congestions and visceral obstructions, with various diseases depending thereon, particularly hæmorrhoids, bilious derangements, bilious and gastric fevers, inflammations, affections of the heart, apoplexy and paralysis, derangements of the stomach and liver, hæmatemesis, affections of the joints, as gout and rheumatism; diseases of the urinary organs, hysteria and uterine disorders, hypochondriasis, and affections of the mind."—COOPER.

Lungs.—The *lungs* gradually lose their elasticity and increase in density; the air cells and bronchi become dilated; hence emphysema and chronic bronchitis, so often seen in the very aged.

We now come to the organs of *secretion* and *digestion.*

Salivary Glands.—To commence with the *salivary glands.* We find that they are hardened and ossified; their bulk in many cases decreases with age; the saliva is either secreted in so small a quantity that food is only partially moistened in the mouth, and swallowed with difficulty, or it is secreted in large quantities, running, or "dribbling," continually from the mouth in the very aged, its composition being altered, in containing more water than normal.

Stomach.—In the stomach, the gastric juice (the use of which is to dissolve the various kinds of foods, reducing the albuminous and fibrinous portions of it to a state fit for absorption into the system), is secreted in a diluted form, and is deficient in pepsin; thus the first process of digestion is improperly carried out. Moreover, the muscular walls of the stomach gradually lose their wonted contractility, the peristaltic motions become weak, and the chyme, or product of the gastric digestion, is feebly transmitted through the pyloric orifice to the intestinal tube, instead of passing in a more vigorous manner, as it does in the prime of life.

Liver.—The *liver*, besides effecting important changes in certain constituents of the blood during its circulation through the gland, is also the secreting organ by which the *bile* is formed. The bile is separated from the blood by the hepatic cells, and is discharged into small ducts, which unite, and terminate in the *ductus communis choledochus.* Its chief purpose is to separate the chyle from the chyme. In old age the minute bloodvessels become hardened and diminished in calibre ; the hepatic cells become indurated, and therefore their secretion becomes slightly altered ; but this alteration differs in degree according to the amount of venous congestion, so often met with in advanced life, and which is caused by the induration, or hardening, of the organ, not allowing that amount of dilatation which existed in the earlier periods of life.

" Diseases of the liver very seldom occur until after puberty." But in after life how few are free from some congestive or structural disorder of the organ ? In childhood and youth the organ possesses sufficient elasticity to allow any increased flow of blood to pass, but in old age the hardened and ossified tunnels will not and cannot dilate ; the veins of the abdomen and lower limbs receive the pressure, and become varicose.

In old age fatty matters are not thoroughly emulsified, or absorbed by the lacteals ; this may be due to an alteration in the fluid secreted by the *pancreas.*

Intestines.—In the intestines the small vessels which supply the follicles and various glands, become indurated, or even " clogged up," in old age ; the walls of the intestines become opaque, and lose their contractility ; the *villi* containing the *lacteals* undergo the same gradual alteration, the latter of which having coats which year by year become less pervious, less and less nourishment is absorbed into the system. From these alterations in the digestive organs, we see, firstly, that food is improperly digested ; secondly, that the chyle, or nutrient part of it, is only partially absorbed by the lacteals ; further, that these defects of function are caused by a gradual process of induration and ossification.

Testes.—In old age the *testes* shrink and nearly disappear ; the spermatic fluid is altered in composition and gradually lost, whilst from a gradual induration and ossification, the vessels of the *erectile* tissues no longer admitting of dilatation, the function of the latter as such is lost.

As age advances, the *prostate* gland is disposed to become enlarged ; and " its ducts often contain small rounded concretions, about the size of a millet seed, which are composed of carbonate of lime and animal matter."

Cowper's glands appear to diminish in old age.

Uterus.—" From the gradual *effects* of *age* alone, independent of impregnation, the uterus shrinks, and becomes paler in colour and *harder in texture ;* its triangular form is lost ; the body and neck become less distinguishable from each other ; the orifices become less characteristic."—QUAIN.

Ovaries.—The same consolidation applies to the *ovaries*, in which Dr. Martin Barry has shown a *large number* of microscopic ovisacs to exist. Nevertheless, the Graafian vesicles approach the surface of the ovary and burst, the ovum and fluid contents of the vesicle passing into the Fallopian tube, *periodically*, from about fifteen, only up to about forty-five to fifty years of age, after which period of life, owing to a hardened and ossified state of the ovary, the vesicles are unable to approach the surface of the organ; *they exist,* but they are imprisoned, their development is arrested, they shrink or disappear; the powers of regeneration and reproduction are therefore lost.

The *urinary organs* are modified by the same consolidation. In the tubuli uriniferi and pelvis of the kidney, calculi are frequently found. The bladder becomes firmer, thicker, and less elastic in old age.

In old age, *adipose* and *cellular tissues* are changed. Fatty matters diminish in quantity, become more fluid and deeper in colour. Cellular tissue gradually becomes denser, more fragile, and inelastic, sometimes assuming a fibrous character.

Serous membranes become denser, and ossific deposits are often found in them; their surface also becomes drier in old age than in youth.

Fibrous structures become firmer, tougher, and more rigid, and often ossified.

In old age fibrin and gelatin increase; albumen diminishes. Many secretions become acrid and irritating, and mucous fluid generally increased.

Owing to languor of the circulation and decreased nerve power, the generation of *animal heat* is dimi-

nished, although exhalation and evaporation from the
lungs and skin, both of which lower the temperature
of the body, are not so great in degree in old age as in
youth.

If we inquire into the cause of the senile changes in
the organs of sensation, we find that sight gradually
fails, that hearing, taste, and smell are gradually
altered by this same process of induration and ossification.

Eye.—In the *eye*, in old age, there is diminished
secretion of the aqueous fluid in the anterior chamber,
the cornea becomes less prominent, the pupil becomes
more dilated from lessened nervous sensibility; hence
distant sight, and the indistinct and confused view of
near objects in the aged.

"Extreme age is a strong predisposing cause to
amaurosis."—MIDDLEMORE.

"It is most frequent at and after the middle period
of life."—LAWRENCE.

"The state of the retina, when examined after
death, in amaurotic eyes, accords with these views . . .
it has been found thickened, opaque, spotted, buff-
coloured, tough, and in some cases even ossified."—
COOPER.

"One case (of amaurosis) very analogous to
amblyopia* senilis, is believed to depend upon a
diminution of the pigmentum nigrum, which secretion,
in some individuals earlier and more considerably, in
others later and in a slighter degree, *recedes with other*

* Amblyopia (from ἀμβλὺς, dull ; ὤψ, the eye). Hippocrates
means by this word the dimness of sight to which *old people* are
subject.—"Aph.," 31, sect. 3.

secretions of a different nature."—BEER's "Lehre von den Augenkr.," b. ii. p. 451.

"In form, colour, degree of transparency, and density, the lens presents marked differences at different periods of life. In the *adult,* the anterior surface of the lens becomes less convex than the posterior, and the substance of the lens firmer (than in childhood), colourless, and transparent. In *old age,* it is flattened on both surfaces, it assumes a yellowish or amber tinge, and is apt to lose its transparency as it gradually increases in toughness and specific gravity."
—QUAIN.

"*Old age* may be regarded as one of the predisposing causes to cataract, inasmuch as the disease is most frequent in advanced life."—COOPER.

"If common senile cataract be not caused by death of the lens, if this explanation of its opacity be rejected, we are totally at a loss to explain its frequent occurrence in aged persons. It is evidently *not produced in them by inflammation,* for it takes place first, it is perceived, in the *centre* of the lens; it occurs in old feeble persons, and is *unattended by pain,* or by any morbid effect in the other parts of the eye, which can with propriety be referred to inflammation."—MIDDLEMORE, "Dis. of Eye."

"On this point, I should say that there is evidence rather of disorganisation, or of alteration in texture, or of a *new deposit* in the lens, than of actual death of it."—COOPER's "Surg. Dic.," art. "Eye."

"Cataract is often suspected to arise from defective *nutrition* of the lens; some imperfection of the nerve, it is conceived, *may be* concerned."—MACKENZIE.

"The cataract of *old people* generally attacks *both eyes*, within the period of a few months; but in *middle life* we often meet with it in *one eye*, the other having continued unaffected for many years."— MACKENZIE.

In *middle life* cataract may be due to some inflammatory action, and only affect *one eye*, but *true senile cataract* is not caused by death of the lens, is not due to any inflammatory action; but there *is a new deposit* in the lens, which accompanies, or is part of, that gradual induration and ossification found in *old age;* therefore *both* eyes are affected at about the same period.

In old age the cornea becomes altered in shape, hardened, or even opaque; the sclerotic undergoes the same modifications, and in some cases is even found ossified. To show that ossification sometimes exists, and is possible, we quote a few extreme cases.

"Scarpa dissected an eye, which was almost entirely transformed into a *stony substance.* It was taken from the body of an *old woman,* and was not above half as large as the sound one. The cornea appeared dusky, and, behind it, the iris of a singular shape, concave, and without any pupil in its centre. The rest of the eyeball, from the limits of the cornea backward, was unusually hard to the touch. The particulars of the dissection of this case will be read with interest in Scarpa's treatise on 'Diseases of the Eye.' Haller met with a similar case (see 'Obs. Pathol. Oper. Min.,' obs. 15). Fabricius Hildanus, Lancisi, Morgagni, Morand, Zinn, and Pellier, make distinct mention of calculi in the interior of the eye. Ossification of the

2—2

capsule of the lens, of that of the vitreous humour, and of, what was supposed to be, the hyaloid membrane, are noticed by Mr. Wardropp."—Cooper, "Surg. Dict."

Mr. Wardropp also mentions an instance of ossification of the cornea. In this case the whole eye was altered in form, and the cornea was opaque; in it a piece of bone weighing two grains, oval-shaped, hard, and with a smooth surface, was found between its lamellæ; ossification of the choroid coat and retina was also found. According to the same authority, Walter had in his museum a piece of cornea taken from a man sixty years of age, containing a bony mass which was three lines long, two broad, and weighed two grains.

Many of the above cases are undoubtedly the result either of accident or some inflammatory action; we must not, therefore, consider them as a natural formation : but in old age, we have sufficient evidence to show that the whole structure of the eye is slightly altered, that the solid parts are hardened, and even ossified; parts which in the earlier periods of life were transparent, become opaque; owing to senile changes in the bloodvessels, the humours (which are secreted) are slightly altered in quantity, colour, and transparency; further, that the retina loses its sensibility owing to the changes in the brain and nerves, which have been already considered.

These changes in the eye, caused, firstly, by a gradual process of solidification and ossification, secondly, by diminished nervous sensibility, fully account for cataract, amaurosis, and other diseases of the eye, becoming more prevalent after the middle period of life, and still more frequent in old age. On the other hand, on the same principle that some persons are gifted with genius in one form or other, a being may be blessed with organs of sight possessing tone and nervous sensibility higher and greater in degree than those of the majority of mankind, and may live to a good old age " with eye not dim." But even then his sight is not so clear, precise, or perfect, as it was in the earlier periods of life. It has undergone the same alterations as those found in other individuals ; these may be slight—it is but a difference in degree.

Ear.—The *ear* is subject to the same gradual process of ossification. The cartilages of the *external ear* become hardened, or even ossified ; the ceruminous glands, which secrete the ear-wax, undergo the same alterations which have been observed in other glands ; the secretion becomes less, and is altered in quality. The membrana tympani becomes thickened and indurated ; the ligaments connecting the ossicles (malleus, incus, and stapes) become hardened—their pliability is lessened ; thus vibrations which are already imperfect, owing to induration of the membrana tympani, are improperly conveyed by the ossicles across the cavity of the tympanum, by means of the internal ear (the structures and fluids of which have undergone the same process of consolidation*), to the auditory nerve, the sensibility of which decreases with the senile changes of the brain. Hence the impaired and confused hearing so often observed in aged persons.

* Fluid in the internal cavities is diminished, or even absorbed, in old age.

Tongue—Taste.—The tongue, besides being the organ of the special sense of taste, also possesses in a very high degree that of touch; these sensitive powers are confined to the membrane which covers it, the upper surface of which is studded all over with numerous sensitive papillæ; in old age, from a gradual loss of nervous susceptibility, also from induration of the bloodvessels supplying these papillæ, their sensibility is diminished. The whole membrane covering the tongue is hardened and thickened, its surface becomes dry and furrowed, and the sense of taste is diminished.

Smell.—In the nose, like the ear, the cartilages which determine its shape become hardened and even slightly ossified; the power of contraction and expansion of the nostrils during respiration, so often observed in the child, is not utilised. Internally, the Schneiderian or pituitary membrane becomes hardened and thickened, the vessels supplying it become indurated and lessened in calibre, and the secretion from the glandular follicles either becomes less, accounting for that dryness of the nose so often observed in the aged, or it becomes watery and increased in quantity, giving rise to symptoms also characteristic of the same. Moreover, the fibres of the *olfactory*, the special nerve of the sense of smell, gradually lose their wonted susceptibility, hence the sense of smell decreases with age; its peculiar power of protecting the lungs from the inhalation of obnoxious gases, and in helping the organs of taste to discriminate the characters of food, is indifferently carried out.

Touch.—We now come to the sense of touch, and as its principal seat is the skin, we will at the same time consider the senile changes in the latter, which is also important as an organ of excretion and absorption.

" The skin consists of two* layers, the derma or cutis vera, and the epidermis or cuticle. On the surface of the former are the sensitive papillæ; and within, or imbedded beneath it, are the sweat-glands, hair follicles, and sebaceous glands." The cutis, or true skin, consists of two layers, the *corium* and *papillary layer*. The latter contains the expansions of the sensitive nerves, and consists of numerous small, highly sensitive, and vascular eminences, which rise perpendicularly from its surface, forming the essential element of the organ of touch.

The average length of these papillæ is about the one-hundredth of an inch; but they are of larger size, and more fully developed upon the palmar surface of the hands, and the plantar surface of the feet. Each papilla contains one or more nerve-fibres, and in parts where the sense of touch is most highly developed, these nerve-fibres seem to be connected with small oval bodies, termed " tactile corpuscles," which Wagner describes as resembling minute fir-cones, and considers them an apparatus subservient to the sense of touch; and it is yet an open question whether or not these bodies develop electricity, and acting as independent and separate ganglia, convey impressions to the brain; but it is out of place to enter upon the subject here; we must therefore content ourselves by inquiring into the senile changes in the skin and organs of touch.

* Some authors give three layers—cuticle, rete mucosum, and cutis vera.

In the first place, in old age the sensibility of the nerves is diminished; the capillaries supplying each papilla are gradually lessened in calibre, or even obliterated. From these two causes the sense of touch is not so perfect in old age as in earlier life. Further, as in other glands the secretions of the sweat and sebaceous glands is diminished; the skin becomes dry, shrunken, and leather-like; it has a cracked or furrowed appearance, especially noticeable where any flexion of joints takes place, or where wasting of the soft parts under the skin causes it to "pucker up." Hence the wrinkles of old persons. In old age, the skin contains more earthy salts than in youth.

Teeth.—A human being is provided with two sets of teeth. The first, or temporary set, make their appearance in childhood, and are developed during fœtal life from the mucous membrane covering the edges of the maxillary arches, by means of papillæ, one for each tooth, which become enclosed by means of a convergence and union of the sides of the primitive dental groove. These papillæ, or pulps, are supplied with bloodvessels and nerves. They gradually enlarge and assume the form of the future teeth, when a gradual process of ossification, or the formation of dentine, commences. A thin osseous shell, or cap of dentine, appears on the points of the pulps; this increases, and eventually takes up its whole substance. At the same time the outer surface of the crown becomes covered with enamel, which is formed from a substance lying on the pulp and adapted to its surface; not by secretion, but by a process analogous to ossification, or a deposition of earthy matter; and we have reason to

believe that the beautiful arrangement of this earthy
matter, as seen in the minute, wavy, branching tubes
lying parallel to each other, in the dentine, measuring
about one four thousand five hundredth part of an inch
in diameter, and the minute hexagonal rods in the
enamel, measuring about one five thousand five hundredth part of an inch in diameter, is due to these
earthy salts being deposited from minute pre-existing
tubules.   The same process still continuing, the root,
or fang, is formed, elongates, and the tooth cuts the
gum about six or seven months after birth, the temporary teeth being completed by the beginning of the
third year.   The temporary teeth begin to fall out at
seven or eight years of age ; these are replaced by the
permanent teeth, which are likewise developed before
birth (with the exception of the last molars), but which
during childhood are lodged in pedunculated cells in
the bone.

The eruption of the permanent teeth commences at
about seven or eight years, and with the exception of
the wisdom teeth, is completed at thirteen or fourteen
years, the latter appearing between seventeen and
twenty-five.   During this time the jaw increases in
depth and length.

In the interior of the bony part of each tooth is a
cavity, which descends or ascends, as the case may be,
into the root, and thereby communicates with the
outer surface.   It contains a delicate vascular membrane, which is called the pulp of the tooth, and is
supplied with bloodvessels and nerves; and although
the bloodvessels send no branches into the hard substance of the teeth, the tubules of the dentine imbibe,

and convey nutrient fluid to it. In support of this the teeth are often stained yellow in jaundice ; and in *young* animals fed on madder, the dentine is often tinged with its colour, but in *older* animals under the same circumstances this colouring does not take place.

As age advances, the bloodvessels supplying the pulp of the teeth indurate and lessen in calibre ; earthy matter increases in the cavity of the tooth, which cavity therefore decreases in size, in old teeth becoming almost obliterated. The blood supply to the tooth is gradually cut off, little by little it loses its nourishment ; its crown becomes worn away by the almost constant process of mastication ; it is not replaced by growth from the root ; the tooth decays, and falls out.

Hair.—Hair is made up of an outer, cortical, horny, or fibrous substance, which invests it, and an inner medullary, or pith-like substance, within ; the latter is made up of a series of cells filled with pigment ; the bulb, or root, is inserted into the skin in what is termed a hair *follicle,* at the bottom of which is a small vascular eminence—a papilla, by means of which material is supplied for the production and constant growth of the hair, blastema being thrown out, in which nucleated cells arise ; these flatten out, unite, and form the fibres which compose the fibrous part of the hair. Many of these cells contain pigment which gives the different characteristic shades to the hair. Thus one hair grows, is nourished and coloured from the blood, through the agency and powers of selection of a single papilla.

Whatever tends to lessen or cut off the supply of blood to this papilla, robs the hair of its powers of growth, nourishment, and colour. During thought, hard study, or mental worry, there is an increased flow of blood to the brain at the expense of that supplying the surface; the hair loses, at all events temporarily, part of its nourishment; hence premature greyness and baldness. Again, during fright, owing to intense contractions of the bloodvessels caused by the action of the sympathetic nerves, the supply of blood is taken away from these papillæ supplying the hair; by this means many persons have become grey, or even partially bald, in a single night. But there is another important change which we have to consider— that is, the process of induration and ossification, which gradually lessens, or even entirely obstructs, the supply of blood to these papillæ, by which means the hair, little by little, loses its powers of growth, nourishment, and colour.

Thus in old age the hair is no longer nourished, it loses its colour—becomes grey or white, for lack of pigment; some of the papillæ are even totally deprived of their blood supply; therefore the bulb shrivels and shrinks, the hair falls away.

In the foregoing pages we have pointed out the differences existing between youth and old age. In the former the various organs and structures are elastic, yielding, and pliable; the senses are keen, the mind active. In the latter, these qualities are usurped by hardness, rigidity, and ossification; the senses are wanting in susceptibility, the mind in memory and capacity.

Further, that these changes are due, firstly, to a gradual accumulation of fibrinous and gelatinous substances; secondly, to a gradual deposition of earthy compounds, chiefly phosphate and carbonate of lime. These, acting in concert, diminish the calibre of the larger arterial vessels, and by degrees partially, and sometimes fully, obliterate the capillaries. By these depositions every organ and structure in the system is altered in density and function; the fluid, elastic, pliable, and active state of body gives place to a solid, inactive, rigid, ossified, and decrepit condition. The whole system is "choked up;" the curtain falls, the play of life is ended, terminating in so-called "natural death."

The general impression is that this accumulation of fibrinous, gelatinous, and osseous matter, is the *result* of old age—the result of time, the remote *effects* of the failure of that mysterious animal principle—life. But in an after chapter we shall show that this great vital principle, which is centred in the cerebro-spinal axis, gradually wanes, because the brain and nerves by degrees lose their supply of blood, their powers of selection and imbibition, and are deprived of their ordained nourishment by means of this gradual process of induration and ossification.

Another prevailing idea is that the embryo, at its first period of existence, is endowed with a certain allotment of vitality—of life, the powers of which perfect the organs and structures of the body, and gradually decline, exhausting itself till death, and that the greater the amount and degree of the numerous uses it is put to, the sooner and more rapidly will existence collapse. The more luminous the flame, the sooner will it be extinguished !

To this idea there are many objections, which would cause us to throw it aside. In many diseases how often is the sunbeam of life, nearly extinguished, known to recover, and shine again, perhaps more brilliantly than before! If we ask its source, can parents, whose supply of vitality is decreasing, give more than they possess to their offspring, and yet keep a portion to themselves?

Vitality emanates from the parent, but there is no doubt that instead of experiencing a diminution, it increases up to a certain period of life, when its maximum grade is attained, after which period the manifestations and functions of life gradually decline. For this decline nature gives a reason, and tells man it is in his power to arrest and curb the causes.

Every organ and structure of the body, up to a certain period of life, possesses, *per se*, the power of reproducing any waste in structure or composition, under favourable circumstances; but after this period, the bloodvessels, which supply without exception every part of the body, become so indurated, hardened, and ossified, that their powers of irrigating and nourishing the different structures decline; the waste is therefore greater than the renewal.

By a simple method of inquiry, we have asked the cause of the differences between youth and old age? Why the various functions of the body are taken away? Why we become old and die?

Nature has answered us.

Induration and ossification are the *causes* of "*old age*" and "*natural death*." And upon this fact will arise the important question, Can we prolong life?

CHAPTER II.

THE SOURCE OF THE ACCUMULATIONS WHICH CAUSE "OLD AGE" AND "NATURAL DEATH."

WE will now inquire into the *source* of these deposi-tions, which gradually accumulate from the first period of existence to old age. Firstly, we will ask the source of the fibrinous and gelatinous substances; secondly, the source of the earthy deposits.

Oxygen is the most abundant of the elements; it forms eight-ninths of water, nearly one-fourth of the air, and about one-half of the chief constituents of the earth's surface.

In the air it exists, in combination chiefly with nitrogen, in the proportions as under :

Oxygen   .   .   .   22
Nitrogen   .   .   .   78
_____
100

In a free state, *nitrogen* is comparatively *inactive;* but *oxygen,* although constituting only a comparatively small proportion of the atmosphere, is the *active* element.

Oxygen combines with all the known elements, with the exception of fluorine, forming oxides. Of that which is chemical in the animal economy, oxygen has perhaps the most important action, whether it be directly chemical, or chemical agency in action and reaction.

During respiration by the lungs, animals inhale the oxygen of the air, and expire or breathe out carbonic acid gas.

A middle-sized man consumes a little over 40,000 cubic inches of oxygen per day, by respiration. This oxygen being positive electricity, creates, or generates, a nitro-hydrogen, or negative action, at the skin and external surfaces. The lungs, heart, and vessels of the arterial system have therefore a positive action, whilst the skin, veins, and liver have a correlative, or negative action. This is chemical agency in action and reaction.

During life, every being throughout animated nature is in a constant state of change—waste by oxygen, renewal by food. The arteries, we may say, distribute oxygen universally, as a cause of the waste, whilst the veins absorb nitrogen, carbon, etc., as the products of that waste, thus giving rise to the union of oxygen with carbon, and to the expiration of carbonic acid gas.

The expiration of carbonic acid is therefore due to oxidation, or waste, of the substances of the body, which oxidation, together with that of the constituents of food, is the supposed source of animal heat.

The experiments of Regnault, Reiset, and Magnus, prove that the lungs are not the seat of the *formation* of carbonic acid, but that carbonic acid is expelled from the blood in the lungs, and that oxygen is taken up in its place—that is, that a current of oxygen is conveyed throughout the system in the arterial blood, which in its passage causes waste, or oxidation, in the capillaries, and thus gives rise to the presence of carbonic acid in venous blood.

Atmospheric air in contact with the lungs undergoes a change; its nitrogen is returned free, together with the carbonic acid expelled from the blood, and part of the *oxygen*, taking the place of the carbonic acid, is carried onward in the arterial blood—now changed from the dark purple-red of venous blood to a bright red colour, by the loss of carbonic acid from the blood corpuscles, and their absorption of oxygen— to take part in many of the vital functions and numerous changes in the animal economy, which are so intimately connected with the new and acquired properties of arterial blood.

There are two substances existing in blood— *albumen* and *fibrin*. The following are their component elements :

			Albumen.	Fibrin.
Carbon	.	.	53·5	52·7
Hydrogen	.	.	7·0	6·9
Nitrogen	.	.	15·5	15·4
Oxygen	.	.	22·0	23·5
Sulphur	.	.	1·6	1·2
Phosphorus	.	.	0·4	0·3
			100·0	100·0

From this analysis we see that fibrin contains 1·5 per cent. more oxygen than albumen.

If we make a clear and strained solution of albumen, or white of egg, and place it in a vessel under circumstances which will not allow the admission of atmospheric air, and pass oxygen through it daily for from four to seven days, a whitish film, insoluble in cold water, is found floating on the surface. This substance is analogous in appearance and properties to the fibrin of blood.

Thus we may justly infer that fibrin is an oxide of albumen.

The lacteals absorb the nutrient part of the products of digestion, the *azotised* substances of which exist either in an albuminous or minutely subdivided state,* and from *some cause* fibrin gradually increases in the contents of the absorbent system during its passage from the lacteals to the thoracic duct, from whence it passes into the blood.

" The proportion of fibrin has been supposed to increase as the *lymph* approaches the thoracic duct; thus from the *lumbar* lymphatics of a fasting horse, Gmelin obtained 0·25 per cent. of dry coagulum, and from that of the *thoracic duct* of the same animal, 0·42 per cent."—QUAIN.

" The *chyle,* when taken from the *lacteal vessels,* before they have reached the glands, is generally found to coagulate less firmly than in the more advanced stage of the process."—*Ibid.*

In Dr. Carpenter's " Human Physiology," the

---

* It has been proved by Magendie, Liebig, and others, that gelatin possesses no nutritive value. In the digestion of fibrin, as in its decomposition, " the putrefaction of a small portion causes the solution of the remainder." A certain portion of the fibrin during digestion is decomposed, the remainder gives up part of its oxygen to the decomposition, and becomes true albumen, coagulable by heat.

following relative proportions of fibrin in different parts of the absorbent system are given as under :

In the afferent or peripheral lacteals (from the intestines to the mesenteric glands) . . . . . } Fibrin, *little*, or none.

In the efferent or central lacteals (from the mesenteric glands to the thoracic duct). . . . . } Fibrin, *medium* quantity.

In the thoracic duct . . . . . { Fibrin, *maximum* quantity.

Thus from *some cause* fibrin increases in the absorbent system, and as we have shown that oxygen will convert albumen (which exists in the lacteals) into fibrin, we may justly infer that oxygen is the *cause* of this increase.

Precisely the same process cf oxidation goes on in the blood, which contains about seven per cent. of albumen ; this is gradually oxidised in the lungs and vessels, and converted into fibrin.

If we partially suspend the respiratory functions, therefore the process of oxidation in the lungs, the amount of fibrin is decreased in the blood, or, more correctly speaking, it is not formed to the same extent.

M. Dupuy found that "when the pneumogastric nerves were divided in the cervical region in horses, the quantity of fibrin in the blood became progressively diminished to a very remarkable extent."

Albuminous substances are being almost continually absorbed by the lacteals and poured into the blood ; thus the supply is kept up, to be little by little converted into fibrin, which is kept in solution in the blood, so long as a certain amount of heat exists, and motion or circulation is given to it. This motion is decreased during circulation through the capillaries. Although much of the fibrin either oozes through their walls, and is deposited to nourish organs and structures and repair their waste, much of it accumulates, lessening the calibre of vessels, and indurating organs and structures. This accumulation is small, the blood usually containing only about three per cent. of fibrin, but it is gradual and constant.

In old age, as well as fibrin, a large quantity of *gelatin* has accumulated.

Gelatin is never found in vegetables, *nor does it exist in the blood*, but it is found in the animal economy, in which it must therefore be *formed.**

Its composition is—carbon, 50; hydrogen, 7; nitrogen, 18; oxygen, 25. It therefore contains 1·5 per cent. more oxygen than fibrin. As fibrin is an oxide of albumen, so is gelatin an oxide of fibrin, and the large quantities existing in old age are due to the action of atmospheric *oxygen* on fibrin deposited from

* In the egg we see an instance of this transformation ; albumen exists, what little fibrin there is being confined to the membranes, but there is *no gelatin.* In the *chick*, on hatching (a process which may be accomplished artificially, by the simple presence of heat, moisture, and atmospheric air), the amount of fibrin is found to have increased, and gelatin is found in comparatively large quantities. In the egg the former was found in minute quantities, the latter not at all. Where do they come from ? Nothing has entered the egg from without but' moisture and air containing *oxygen.* The action of oxygen on albumen is the cause.

the blood. If we carry the process of oxidation still further, we find that part of these fibrinous and gelatinous substances are decomposed as the waste of tissues, and resolved into the compounds of ammonia and urea, and eliminated from the system ;* but at the same time the gradual process of accumulation is going on; it is a battle between accumulation and removal. The former is the victor and gains the upper hand ; hence the accumulation is greater than the elimination.

Thus the *fibrinous* and *gelatinous* accumulations found in old age, are *caused by* the action of that never-resting, active, corroding, and destroying element, atmospheric *oxygen.*

The *earthy salts,* which we have already pointed out increase with age, are found by experiment to exist in different proportions in different individuals of the same age, which leads us to the conclusion that these depositions arise from various causes, or, if from the same cause, variable in intensity. On the inner surface of an ordinary tea-kettle, after being regularly used for several months, a considerable amount of incrustation has taken place; and although it is generally believed that this incrustation arises from the deposi-

---

* "If ten eqs. of oxygen be added to albumen, a formula will be given containing the elements of the membranes and choleic acid."—LIEBIG.

Further, that when uric acid is formed from gelatin, the elements of choleic acid (an important acid of the bile) remain, and we are of opinion that, at no late period, the formation of many of the complex constituents of the urine and bile, from substances originating from albumen, by the presence of a certain amount of heat, and by the simple additions of water and oxygen, will be demonstrably correct.

tion of earthy substances from the water, consequent upon boiling,* and rendering *insoluble* the previously *soluble* salts of lime, experiment shows that the great bulk of this incrustation arises from matter previously soluble being precipitated, in consequence of the water which held it in solution being driven off in the form of steam, and the water remaining in the vessel being thus more than saturated, the excess is thrown down.

Here we have a condition precisely similar to that which exists in the living human body, as the process of transpiration. Transpiration is nothing more or less than the evaporation and elimination of the fluids and gases of the system.

The basis of animal fluids is water, and these fluids hold certain compounds of lime in solution; and when, by transpiration, the watery basis is eliminated (precisely as in the common tea-kettle), a portion of these lime compounds are, and must be, deposited. And although much of the matter deposited is carried off in the *excretæ*, much also is left behind in the different organs and structures of the body, which, little by little

---

* The general impression is that *hard* water is caused by the presence of carbonate of lime, held in solution by an excess of carbonic acid gas, and that on boiling the latter is eliminated, and the carbonate, being no longer soluble, is precipitated. This is, however, an error. Carbonates are not the cause of hard water, which state is due to the presence of sulphate of lime, or soluble gypsum. Thus, on washing with soap in hard water, a chemical decomposition takes place; the sulphuric acid of the sulphate of lime unites with the soda of the soap, forming sulphate of soda, which remains in solution, whilst the lime unites with the tallow, forming oleate and stereate of calcium, an insoluble compound which floats on the surface of the water.

increasing, form accumulations which bring the individual to that stage of "old age" and decrepitude
which terminates in "natural death."

In the lungs, "the air-tubes, after repeated divisions
and sub-divisions, terminate in small vesicular cells,
on the walls of which a minute capillary network of
bloodvessels is distributed. The membrane which
constitutes these cells, and through which the atmosphere acts upon the blood, is believed to be at least
thirty times as extensive as the surface of the body.
The lungs, therefore, constitute one vast *excreting* surface, from which is constantly escaping into the air a
mixed *cloud* of carbonic acid, gas, and *water.*"—
HOOPER's "Physician's Vade Mecum."

The quantity of water exhaled from the lungs,
according to the average estimates of different authorities, amounts to from seven ounces to one pint eleven
ounces in the twenty-four hours.

Thus the lungs eliminate carbonic acid gas, water,
and other *volatile* substances. *Earthy salts* are not
volatile, and are therefore *not eliminated by the lungs.*

The *skin* eliminates chiefly *water* and carbonic acid,
also nitrogen, lactate and acetate of ammonia, and a
small quantity of alkaline and *earthy salts.*

"It is calculated that about *three pounds of water*
are daily conveyed to the surface as insensible perspi-
ration." This is, however, increased during hot
weather and by exercise.

The purpose of the *urine* is to remove a portion of
the liquid and solid matters which have been taken
into the system as food, also to carry off materials
resulting from the waste or disorganisation of tissues.

It is secreted by the kidneys from arterial blood, and contains in the thousand parts, on an average, nine hundred and fifty of water, the remaining fifty parts being composed of *organic* constituents—urea, uric, lithic, hippuric, and lactic acids; salts of ammonia and extractive matters; and *inorganic* constituents—carbonic, sulphuric, hydrochloric, and phosphoric acids, combined with soda, potash, magnesia, and lime. If we remove the water and collect one thousand parts of the solid matters, they are found to contain, on an average, sixteen parts, or 1·6 per cent. of *earthy* salts. Lehmann's analysis gives 1·5 per cent.

The *solids* discharged in the urine in twenty-four hours average less than one and a half ounces; taking this, however, as an average, about twenty-one grains of earthy salts are daily eliminated by the kidneys; but a portion of the phosphates in the urine is secreted in the mucus of the bladder.

The amount of earthy salts in fæces excreted in the twenty-four hours is generally about one-fourth of the quantity voided in the urine, or a little more than five grains,* a small quantity of which is perhaps derived from the saliva and other secretions of digestion, the rest from articles taken into the system as diet, and on which the amount depends.

Owing to the many different conditions of quantity and quality of foods, hard and soft water, excretion by the skin and kidneys being increased by activity and hard work, and decreased inversely, thus varying in the amount of solid constituents according to the specific gravity of the urine, which alters slightly even

* This item varies considerably, and is frequently very much larger.

hourly, it is impossible to collect a correct average of the amount of earthy salts taken into the system, and the amount excreted by it, from the many different authors, or even to obtain the same by *occasional* observation. We therefore determined to experiment on ourselves, by carefully weighing the amount of solids and measuring the amount of liquids consumed, and calculating as minutely as possible, from the observations of well-authenticated analysts, and from our own made at the time, the amount of earthy matter they contained—*i.e.* the amount taken into the system; and also by analysing and weighing the amount of earthy compounds carried off by the different excretæ. To avoid error, these experiments were carried on for some weeks, and always gave the same result: that *the amount taken into the system was greater than the amount eliminated.** This amount fluctuated daily, sometimes amounting to mere traces in the twenty-four hours. But if we multiply even traces by days and years, we find a considerable amount of earthy salts unaccounted for. We have already shown that they exist in larger quantities in the body in old age than in middle life, and in the latter than in childhood. They *are*, therefore, *retained and deposited in the system*, and little by little increasing, give rise to the changes observed as age advances.

On removing the water from blood, and incinerating its solid constituents, 1·25 to 1·5 per cent. of ash is left. This is composed of hydrochlorate of soda and

---

* The experiments of Boussingault, on horses, confirm this in animals.

potash, carbonates and phosphates of soda, sulphate of potash, *phosphate of lime and magnesia, carbonates of lime and magnesia,* and peroxide of iron.

According to the analysis of M. Le Canu, for which he gained the prize given by the Académie Royale de Médecine of Paris, the compounds of lime, magnesia, and iron constitute 2·1 in the thousand parts of liquid human blood.

Thus in blood are certain proportions of calcareous matter.

As the *blood* is built up from the *chyle* (which is formed from the chyme by the action of the bile and pancreatic fluid), we should expect to find in the latter the same calcareous matter ; *and such is the fact,* that, on analysis, we find the same earthy salts in the chyle as exist in the blood.

As the *chyle* is formed from the *chyme* (which is the product of the action of the stomach and its secretions on food), we should in it find the same calcareous matter ; and such, again, is the *fact.*

But as the *chyme* is the product of *digestion,* we expect to find the same calcareous matter in the contents of the stomach ; and such also is the *fact.*

The contents of the stomach consist of food and drink taken to nourish and support the system, and in that food and drink we ought to find the same calcareous substances ; and chemical analysis gives to us the certain answer, that the food and drink taken to support the system contain, besides the elements of nutrition, *earthy salts,* which are the *cause* of ossification, obstruction, old age, and natural death.

We have now traced these earthy compounds which

are found in the system, and which increase as age
advances, to the blood, from which they are, by the
process of transpiration, gradually deposited.   From
the blood we trace them to the chyle, from the chyle to
the chyme, and from the chyme to the contents of the
stomach, and thence to articles of diet.

Thus we eat to live, and eat to die !

As we have traced these earthy salts to our food or
articles of diet, we naturally inquire whether the
different kinds of food and drink, which we have for
our selection, contain the same proportion of ossifying
and " old age " producing matter ?   Here chemical
analysis answers in the negative !   Some of the most
generally used alimentary substances contain a comparatively *large* proportion of earthy compounds, some
a *moderate*, and others a very *small* amount.

No matter what kind of food we eat, or what fluid
we drink, the earthy salts contained therein have all
the same source—the earth.

If we eat vegetable food, plants derive their earthy
salts from the earth in which they grow.   If animal
flesh be our sustenance, they have the same source,
through the medium of the animal we eat, which
derives its supply from vegetation.

Fish in the sea, fowl in the air, animals upon the
earth, all derive the earthy salts contained in them
originally from the earth, in the food on which they live.

Any organ, or all the organs put together, of man
or any being, cannot *generate* any element; hence *all
that is earthy in man is derived from the earth.*

From this it follows, that if we can so regulate our
diet—food and drink—that the amount of earthy

matter taken into the system be sufficient only for the growth and nourishment of the bones, without which our powers of strength and motion would be useless (the body being deprived of its mechanical levers), the many organs and structures would not, and could not, harden and ossify; the arteries would not become indurated and lessened in calibre, capillaries would not become obliterated, the brain would not decrease in size by age, sight would not fail, hearing, taste, and smell would not lose their susceptibility, hair would not turn grey, the skin would not become dry and wrinkled, the body would retain its fluidity, elasticity, and activity, and the brain its mental capabilities.

If we can so regulate our diet that these earthy compounds are taken into the system in *smaller* quantities, and therefore take a *longer* period to accumulate —if we can even partially accomplish this—we can prolong life !

We have shown " old age " and " natural death " to be due to *two* causes—*firstly*, to the action of atmospheric *oxygen,* which consumes our bodies and causes fibrinous and gelatinous accumulations; *secondly*, to a deposition of *earthy* matter (ossification). If, therefore, we can, by artificial means, partially arrest the never-ceasing action of atmospheric oxygen, and at the same time prevent the accumulations of these earthy compounds, or even remove them from the system—that state of body termed " old age " would be deferred, and life would be prolonged for a *lengthened period !*

      *   *   *   *   *   *

" Many of the fundamental or leading ideas of the

present time appear, to him who knows not what science has already achieved, as extravagant as the notions of the alchemists."—LIEBIG.

*   *   *   *   *   *

In all the animal kingdom there is a beauty of structure manifested, wondrous, marvellous, and exquisite; but man *alone* has been endowed with knowledge, wisdom, and understanding, as a sole and exclusive gift to him.

Speaking of the patriarchs,* Josephus affirms: "*Their food was fitter for the prolongation of life;* and besides, God afforded them a longer time of life on account of their virtue, and the good use they made of it in astronomical and geometrical discoveries." Who, therefore, can deny, that with all our knowledge and discoveries, which are daily increasing, man may not again re-discover the secret of long life, which has been lost for so many ages, and which secret may probably be summed up in the following few words:

If a human being subsists upon food which contains a large proportion of lime, a large proportion will

---

* Many authors contend that the years, at the time of the patriarchs, were shorter than at the present time—not more than one-fourth the period. If this were true, Methusaleh would have lived only two hundred and forty-three years, Terah fifty-one, and Abram forty-four. Enoch would have been only sixteen when he begat Methusaleh, Arphaxad eight and three-quarters when he begat Salah, Salah seven years old when he begat Eber, and Adam would have been more than a great-grandfather at thirty-three. There is no evidence to show the years were less than at the present time. It is probable, and quite possible (presuming that their diet tended to longevity), that the patriarchs lived to their recorded ages.

enter into the composition of the chyme, the chyle, and the blood; and as from the blood the deposition of lime takes place, the greater the amount of lime that blood contains, the greater will be the amount deposited in the system, the greater the degree of ossification, and the sooner will be produced that rigidity, inactivity, and decrepitude, which makes him old and brings him to *premature death*.

On the other hand, if the food and drink taken to nourish and support the body are selected from the articles which contain the *least* amount of lime, the least amount will enter into the composition of the chyme, the chyle, and the blood, the less amount will there be to deposit, the less the degree of ossification, the less the rigidity, inactivity, and decrepitude, and the *longer the life of the man !*

CHAPTER III.

DIET IN COMPOSITION AND QUANTITY AS BEST ADAPTED TO A PROLONGED EXISTENCE.

BEFORE entering directly upon the subject of diet and its composition, we venture a few remarks upon the structure and organisation of man, relative to his adaptation for a prolonged existence.

If we view the genus *Homo*, either as a whole or in its divisions, irrespective of colour, climate, or habit, we find a great similarity in both an anatomical and a physiological sense. The structure, organisation, and functions are the same in one and all. The body of man is perfect, its Creator " saw that it was good ;" the same Creator gave to man wisdom, and it is a duty to that Creator to use such wisdom in gaining knowledge, which will enable him to keep that body perfect.

" Like the pious pilgrim to the Holy Land, toil on in search of the sacred shrine, in search of truth—God's truth, God's laws—as manifested in His works, in His creation."—H.R.H. THE LATE PRINCE CONSORT.

" The human body, as a machine, is perfect . . . it is apparently intended to go on for ever."—DR. MUNRO.

" If we could imagine a physiologist seeing for the first time an organised structure, such as the human frame, in a state of perfection, however closely he might examine it, and however intimately he might know the structure, he could not, without the knowledge of experience, pretend to say there appeared any reason why death should occur; he could not, indeed, conceive such a thought as death."—DR. REDFORD.

" Such a machine as the human frame, unless accidentally depraved, or injured by some external cause, would seem formed for perpetuity."—" Medical Conspectus," DR. GREGORY.

" If a living organised being be examined at the epoch of its greatest perfection . . . a mutuality of cause and effect is perceived which almost promises immortality."—SIR T. C. MORGAN.

" At some future day there can be little doubt that the value and duration of life will be *extended* greatly beyond what it is at present—*greatly beyond*, perhaps, *what we at present can imagine.*"—"Medical Dictionary," by Dr. Thomson.

The body is in a constant state of change—of waste and renewal. Oxygen consumes and wastes the many different tissues ; we take food to supply the loss ; in that food we take into the system the elements of destruction—earthy salts. As we have already stated, every organ and structure, up to a certain period of life, has the power of reproducing and repairing any waste, after which period the bloodvessels become so indurated and lessened in calibre, that their powers of irrigating and nourishing the various structures decline. Could these channels be kept free from any obstruction, the brain would act, because the heart would act ; the heart would act, because the brain would act, as a perpetual motion ; the functions would maintain the organisation ; the renewal would be equal to the waste and decay ; there would be a harmony and mutuality of cause and effect, and man, could this be effected, would have an existence almost promising immortality.

We are not justified in putting a *limit* to the days of man ; science fails to prove one, religion does not dictate one. The well-known expression, " The days of our years are threescore years and ten," is *not* an *edict* from God, but simply a *lamentation* that the term of life was so reduced by the wickedness and ignorance of the people.

Were it not for the superstitions, prejudices, and tyrannies which kept humanity, as it were, underground ; were it not for the theories and hypotheses which are made to explain phenomena before their cause is known, our knowledge would be of a more rational, purer, and more complete kind; one branch of science would not be constantly waging war against another; the investigations and discoveries of to-day would have no need of contradiction to-morrow; all would be harmony and progression.

Facts, designs, and discoveries, which have been for a time neglected, despised, or ridiculed, one by one arise to reproach ignorance and benefit humanity. These are generally the result of investigation which we are not on any grounds justified in arresting.

"It is perfectly vain to attempt to stop investigation. . . . Depend upon it, if a chemist, by bringing the proper materials together, could produce a human body, he would do it. And why not? There is no command forbidding him to do it; his inquiries are limited solely by his own capacity."—PROF. TYNDAL.

We are justified in carrying our investigations, if they are for the benefit of man, in either mind, body, or estate, to the utmost limit, in the firm belief, and under the true conviction, that "The effort to extend the dominion of man over nature is the most healthy and most noble of all ambitions."—BACON.

When we view the majority of mankind in relation to his diet, our knowledge of his habits and disposition points out to us the many difficulties to be surmounted in ordering any alteration in his predisposed and acquired indulgences; indeed, the difficulties are so great that we are induced to quote the following:

"The common definition of man is false; he is not a reasoning animal. The best you can predicate of

him is, that he is an animal *capable* of reasoning."—
WARBURTON.

This is true in many cases ; it is very true in regard
to his diet.   And further, as Cato observes, "It is a
hard and difficult task to undertake to dispute with
men's stomachs, which have no ears."

Some men have, perhaps, no cares, others pass an
existence which may be a constant scene of trouble ;
but how many of these think there is no other pleasure
in life but in eating, drinking, and sleeping ! Many
men at a certain age become lost to the other enjoyments of life, and these become the only pleasures
they recognise.   This wonderful being of creation,
whose place is to have dominion over all things, dies
—true, he has lived, but in *many* cases he has done no
good to himself ; he has not benefited those around
him, or those that come after him.   Yet he *has lived,*
and expects to be rewarded with a seat in heaven.
For what ?

Surely there is a better purpose in man's existence
than mere eating, drinking, and sleeping, resembling
the life of the lower animals.   Man has a higher destiny
and a nobler purpose ; he should aim to give happiness
to himself and those around him.   He is lord of creation ; let him strive to become its ruler and benefactor.

Many men are ruled and governed by their diet—
their "belly is their God."   Many undertakings are
influenced by the same, whether they be the meeting
of relations and friends for pleasure or for pain, for
marriage or the funeral, commercial transactions, the
meetings of lodges, clubs, or guilds ; societies with the
banner of "Charity" unfurled above them, whether

they be ecclesiastical, constitutional, or benevolent ; meetings for social, agricultural, scientific, judicial, and political purposes ; congresses for peace or war— for the destruction or preservation of men ; all these different assemblies meet in a social and friendly manner. The banquet has become an institution ; even her Majesty's ministers have " YE ANNUALE WHYTEBAITE DINNER, for ye sadde and sobere comforte of frendes, and ye guestes are bydden to eate after ye *Hungarie* mannere."

How many diseases can be traced to over-eating ! How few to moderation or eating little ! When will man, who is *capable* of reasoning, use that reason ? When will he remove the mist from his eyes, which has shrouded them for so many generations ?

When he does this he will see that the *object* of his diet is to keep up a balance between waste and renewal —to give an *equilibrium* to the system.

Before entering further upon the subject, it will be necessary to review the analyses of the most generally used articles of diet, when we shall be able to select from them those best adapted, in composition and quantity, for prolonging existence.

Most of the following analyses are taken from the "Food Collection" in the Bethnal Green Museum, or from the writings of good authorities on the subject. As cereals at the present time constitute the basis of human food, their composition is first given. We must not, however, forget that differences in soil, manure, and culture give rise to variable results ; also, that artificial manures, so largely employed in modern agriculture, alter the quantity of salts, or "ashes," which they contain ; these results are, therefore, only proximately correct.

WHEAT (*Triticum*).

" Good wheat should give three-fourths of its weight of fine flour; but the chemical composition of this depends upon the greater or less quantity which it contains of the outer husks. The finest flour is not so rich in flesh-forming matter as the coarser kinds."

The average composition in one hundred parts may be taken as :

Water	14·0
Gluten	12·8
Albumen	1·8
Starch	59·7
Sugar	5·5
Gum	1·7
Fat	1·2
Fibre	1·7
Ashes	1·6
Total	100·0

BEANS (*Faba vulgaris*).

Water	14·8
Caseine	24·0
Starch	36·0
Sugar	2·0
Gum	8·5
Fat	2·0
Woody fibre	9·2
Mineral matter (ashes)	3·5
Total	100·0

BARLEY (*Hordeum distichum*).

Water	. . .	14·0
Gluten	. . .	12·8
Albumen	. . .	0·0*
Starch	. . .	48·0
Sugar	. . .	3·8
Gum .	. . .	3·7
Fat .	. . .	0·3
Fibre	. . .	13·2
Ashes	. . .	4·2
Total	. . .	100·0

ASH OF BARLEY.

Silica	. . .	29·67
Phosphoric acid	. .	36·80
Sulphuric acid	. .	0·16
Chlorine	. .	0·15
Peroxide of iron	. .	0·83
Lime	. . .	3·23
Magnesia .	. .	4·30
Potash	. . .	16·00
Soda	. . .	8·86
Total	. .	100·00

EINHOFF.

OATS (*Avena sativa*).

" The outer husk of oats, unlike wheat, is poor in flesh-formers, so that oatmeal is better than the whole

° Einhoff gives albumen in barley as 1·15 in 100 parts.

oat as food. In making oatmeal, one quarter of oats (328 lbs.) yields 188 lbs. of meal and 74 lbs. of husks, the rest being water. Oatmeal is remarkable for its large amount of fat."

Water . . .	13·6
Flesh-formers (gluten, albumen, etc.) . . .	17·0*
Starch . . .	39·7
Sugar . . .	5·4
Gum . . .	3·0
Fat . . .	5·7
Fibre . .	12·6
Mineral matter (ashes) . .	3·0
Total . . .	100·0

Rye (*Secale cereale*).

Water . . .	13·00
Gluten . . .	10·79
Albumen . . .	3·04
Starch · . .	51·14
Gum . . .	5·31
Sugar . . .	3·74
Fat . . .	0·95
Woody fibre . .	10·29
Mineral matter (ashes) .	1·74
Total . . .	100·00

* Sibson found gluten in oats to the extent of 11·85 in 100 ; in oatmeal, 15·68 in 100. Vogel gives 4 parts of albumen in 100 of oatmeal.

ULTIMATE ANALYSIS OF WHEAT, RYE, AND OATS, DRIED AT 230° F.

	Wheat.	*Rye.*	*Oats.*
Carbon	46·1	46·2	50·7
Hydrogen	5·8	5·6	6·4
Oxygen	43·4	44·2	36·7
Nitrogen	2·3	1·7	2·2
Ashes	2·4	2·3	4·0
Total	100·0	100·0	100·0

BOUSSINGAULT.

MAIZE, or INDIAN CORN (*Zea Mays*).

Water · . · . · .	14·0
Gluten : . .	12·0
Albumen . . .	0·0*
Starch . · .	60·0
Sugar and Gum . .	0·3
Fat . · . . .	7·7
Fibre . · . . ·	5·0
Mineral matter (ashes) . :	1·0
Total . . .	100·0

RICE (*Orysa sativa*).

Water . . .	13·5
Gluten . . .	6·5
Starch . ′ .	74·1
Sugar . . .	0·4
Gum . . .	1·0
Fat . ′ . . ·	0·7
Fibre . . .	3·3
Mineral matter (ashes) .	0·5
Total . . .	100·0

° Brande gives albumen 2·5; Graham gives the same quantity.

MALT.

Starch	. . .	69·0
Gum .	. . .	14·0
Sugar	. . .	16·0
Gluten	. . .	1·0

Total .	. .	100·0

DR. THOMPSON.

GARDEN BEANS (*Vicia faba*).

Starch .	. .	34·17
Amylaceous fibre	. .	15·89
Legumine (caseine)	· .	10·86
Gum	. .	4·61
Albumen	. . .	0·81
Sweet extractive matter	.	3·54
Membrane .	. .	10·05
Water	. .	15·63
Salts (ashes)	. .	3·46
Loss	. .	0·98

Total .	. .	100·00

EINHOFF.

KIDNEY BEAN (*Phaseolus vulgaris*).

Starch	. .	35·94
Amylaceous fibre	. .	11·07
Legumine (caseine)	.	20·81
Gum	. .	19·37
Albumen	. .	1·35
Sweet extractive	. .	3·41
Membrane .	. .	7·50
Water	. .	(dried)
Salts (ashes)	. .	0·55

Total .	. .	100·00

EINHOFF.

PEAS (*Pisum sativum*).

Water	.	.	. 14·1
Caseine	.	.	. 23·4
Starch	.	.	. 37·0
Sugar	.	.	. 2·0
Gum	.	.	. 9·0
Fat .	.	.	. 2·0
Woody fibre	.	.	10·0
Mineral ashes	.	.	2·5
Total	.	.	. 100·0

Dr. Pereira gives :

Starch	.	.	. 32·45
Amylaceous fibre	.	.	21·88
Legumine (caseine)	.	.	14·56
Gum ·	.	.	. 6·37
Albumen	.	.	. 1·72
Sweet extractive	.	.	2·11
Water	.	.	. 14·06
Salts (ashes)	.	.	. 6·56
Loss	.	.	. ·29
Total	.		100·00

LENTILS (*Ervum lens*). .

" Lentils, like other leguminous seeds, contain much caseine. They are a favourite food in the East. The Hindoo adds lentils to his starch-giving rice, and obtains from them the nourishment the latter does not contain. . . . Lentils are particularly nutritious. . . . The food sold under the name of ' Revalenta Arabica ' is the meal of the lentil after being freed from its outer skin, which [is indigestible. The 'red pottage' for which Esau sold his birthright appears to have been made of lentils. One hundred parts contain, so far as is known :"

Water . . .	14·0
Caseine . . .	26·0
Starch . . .	35·0
Sugar . . .	2·0
Gum . . .	7·0
Fat	2·0
Woody fibre . .	12·5
Mineral matter (ashes) .	1·5
Total . . .	100·0

According to Dr. Pereira, lentils consist of :

Starch . . .	32·81
Amylaceous fibre .	18·75
Legumine (caseine) .	37·32
Gum	5·99
Albumen . . .	1·15
Sweet extractive .	3·12
Water . . .	(dried) ?
Salts . . .	0·57
Loss . . .	0·29
Total . .	100·00

BUCKWHEAT (*Polyponum fagopyrum*).

" Buckwheat is known in this country by the name of ' brank,' and is cultivated for the sake of its green fodder. It is sometimes mixed with wheat-flour.

Birds are exceedingly fond of it, and one of the principal uses made of it in this country is to feed pheasants in the winter."

It consists of :

Water	14·2
Gluten	8·6
Starch	50·0
Gum	2·0
Sugar	2·0
Fat	1·0
Woody fibre	20·4
Mineral matter (ashes)	1·8
Total	100·0

VEGETABLE ROOTS.

Potato (*Solanum tuberosum*).

Water	75·2
Flesh - formers (albumen, gluten, etc.)	1·4
Starch	15·5
Dextrine	0·4
Sugar	3·2
Fat	0·2
Fibre	3·2
Ashes	0·9
Total	100·0

According to Einhoff, the potato contains :

Albumen and mucilage	5·4
Starchy matter	22·0
Water, salts, and loss	72·6
Total	·100·0

Dr. Pereira gives :

Water	66·875
Starch and amylaceous fibre	30·469
Albumen	0·503
Gluten	0·055
Fat	0·056
Gum	0·020
Asparagin	0·063
Extractive	0·921
Chloride of potassium	0·176
Silicate, phosphate, and citrate of iron, manganese, alumina, soda, potash and lime	0·815
Free citric acid	0·047
Total	100·000

PARSNIPS (*Pastinaca sativa*).

Water	82·039
Albumen and caseine	1·215
Sugar	2·882
Starch	3·507
Fat	0·546
Gum	0·748
Woody fibre	8·022
Ashes	1·041
Total	100·000

TURNIPS (*Brassica rapa*).

Water . . .	90·5
Albumen and caseine .	1·1
Sugar . . .	4·0
Gum	1·5
Woody fibre . . .	2·4
Mineral matter (ashes) .	0·5
Total . . .	100·0

According to Dr. Pereira, the turnip contains :

Water . . .	92·5
Solid matter . . .	7·5
Total . . .	100·0

Ultimate composition of dried turnips :

Carbon . . .	42·9
Hydrogen . . .	5·5
Oxygen . . .	42·3
Nitrogen . . .	1·7
Ashes . . .	7·6
Total . . .	100·0

CARROTS (*Daucus carota*).

Water . . .	87·5
Albumen and caseine .	0·6
Sugar . . .	6·4
Fat	0·2
Gum	1·0
Woody fibre . . .	3·3
Mineral matter (ashes) .	1·0
Total . . .	100·0

The *Juice* of the carrot contains :

Fixed oil (some part volatile) .	1· 0
Red crystalline substance (carotin) .	·34
Uncrystallisable sugar, with starch and malic acid . . .	93·71
Albumen	4·35
Ashes (alumina, lime, iron) . .	·60
Total	100· 0

PEREIRA.

SWEET POTATO (*Convolvulus Batatas*).

" The sweet potato is eaten largely in tropical America."

Water . . .	67·50
Starch . . .	16·05
Sugar . . .	20·20
Albumen . . .	1·50
Fat	0·30
Woody fibre . .	0·45
Gum, etc. . . .	1·10
Ashes . . .	2·90
Total . . .	100·00

ONIONS.

Acrid volatile oil,
Uncrystallisable sugar,
Gum,
Vegetable albumen,
Woody fibre,
Acetic and phosphoric acids,
Phosphate and carbonate of lime,
Water.   PEREIRA.

According to Vaquelin and Fourcroy, the onion consists of : A white, acrid, volatile, and odorous oil; sulphur combined with oil, which makes it fœtid. A large quantity of uncrystallisable sugar; a large quantity of mucilage, like gum arabic; a vegeto-animal matter, coagulable by heat and analogous to gluten; phosphoric acid, *in part free*, in part combined with lime; acetic acid; citrate of lime, and a very tender fibrous matter, retaining some vegeto-animal matter.

" Garlic, leeks, and shalots have a similar composition."

OTHER VEGETABLES.

Cabbage.

Extractive matter	.	.	.	. 2·34
Gummy extractive	.	.	.	. 2·89
Resin .	.	.	.	. 0·05
Vegetable albumen	.	.	.	. 0·29
Fecula .	.	.	.	. 0·63
Water, with acetic acid, sulphate and nitrate of potash, chloride of potassium, malate and phosphate of lime, phosphate of magnesia, iron, and manganese .		.	.	. 93·80
Total .	.	.	.	. 100·00

PEREIRA.

According to Sibson, the cabbage contains 1·87 per cent. of inorganic matter (ashes).

" The cabbage, dried, contains 30 to 35 per cent. of gluten."

CAULIFLOWER.

Colouring matter, mucilage, resin, vegetable
    albumen (about)   .   .   .   .   0·5
Chlorophylle, fatty matter, pectic acid (a pro-
    duct ?) woody fibre (about)   .   .   1·8
Water, rather more than   .   .   .   90·0
Silica, malate of ammonia, malate of lime, *free*
    malic acid, acetate of potash, phosphate of
    lime, chloride of calcium, and sulphate of
    potash   .   .   .   .   . traces.

PEREIRA.

" Cauliflower, *dried*, contains gluten, sometimes as.
high as 64 per cent."

ASPARAGUS

consists of :

> Asparagine (asparamide), ·
> Gum,
> Uncrystallisable sugar,
> Vegetable albumen,
> Resin,
> Woody fibre,
> Acetate, malate, phosphate, ˙and muriate of
>   potash, lime, and iron.

CUCUMBER.

"The fresh peel contains solid matters similar to

those of the peeled fruit, but containing much fungus-like matter 15·0, water 85·0, in 100·0."

Green and peeled, the cucumber consists of:

Sugar and extractive	1·66
Chlorophylle	0·04
Odorous matter	?
Fungus-like membrane . . .	?
Soluble albumen	0·13
Phosphate of lime	0·53
Free phosphoric acid, an ammoniacal salt, malate, phosphate, sulphate, and muriate of potash, with sulphate of lime and iron	0·50
Water	97·14
Total	100·00

Mushrooms (*Morels*).

Stearine and elaine	4· 0
Sugar	2· 0
Albumen	1· 2
Azotised extract, or vegetable osmazome .	29· 4
Fungine	39· 6
Gummy azotised extractive . . .	5· 4
Boletate, and phosphate of ammonia and potash	8· 0
Water	10· 0
Total	98·16

BRANDE.

FRUITS.

DATES.

(*The Flesh.*)

Uncrystallisable sugar .	58·0
Pectine . . .	8·9
Gum	3·4
Bassorine . . .	4·1
Fatty matter . . .	0·2
Wax . . .	0·1
Fibre, with traces of colouring matter and tannic acid .	2·3
Water . . .	23·0
Total . . .	100·0

PEREIRA.

(*The Kernel.*)

Fibre . . .	39·6
Gummy matter . .	36·4
Gum and mucus . .	2·5
Epidermis (albumen) .	0·6
An astringent acid (catechu ?)	7·1
Stearine . . .	0·5
Oleine . . .	0·3
Water . . .	13·0
Total . . .	100·0

Ibid.

5

SWEET ALMONDS.

Fixed oil . . .	54·0
Emulsin . . .	24·0
Liquid sugar . .	6·0
Gum . . .	3·0
Seed-coats . . .	5·0
Woody fibre	4·0
Water . . .	3·5
Acetic acid and loss . .	0·5
Total . . .	**100·0**

PEREIRA.

BITTER ALMONDS.

Volatile oil and hydrocyanic acid, quantity undetermined	0·0
Fixed oil . . .	28·0
Emulsin . . .	30·0
Liquid sugar . .	6·5
Gum . . .	3·0
Seed-coats . . .	8·5
Woody fibre . .	5·0
Loss . . .	19·0
Total . . .	**100·0**

Ibid.

FIGS.

Granular sugar (glucose) .	62·5
Fatty matter . . .	0·9
Extractive, with chloride of calcium . . .	0·4
Gum, with phosphoric acid .	5·2
Woody fibre, and *achenia* .	15·0
Water . . .	16·0
Total . . .	**100·0**

Ibid.

GRAPE (*Juice, when ripe*).

Extractive,
Sugar, granular and uncrystallisable,
Gum,
Glutinous matter,
Malic acid (a little),
Citric acid (a little),
Tannic acid,
Bitartrate of potash.

Another analysis (Juice, when ripe).

Odorous matter,
Sugar,
Gum,
Glutinous matter,
Malic acid and malate of lime,
Bitartrate of potash,
Supertartrate of lime.

(*Juice, when unripe.*)

Wax,
Chlorophylle,
Tannin,
Glutinous matter (deposit from the juice),
Extractive,
Sugar (uncrystallisable),
Gallic acid,
Tartaric acid (free), about 1·12 per cent.
Malic acid (free), about 2·19 per cent.
Bitartrate of potash,
Malate, phosphate, sulphate, and muriate of lime.

TAMARIND.

Citric acid . . .	9·40
Tartaric acid . .	1·55
Malic acid . . .	0·45
Bitartrate of potash .	3·25
Sugar . . .	12·50
Gum . . .	4·70
Vegetable jelly, pectine .	6·25
Parenchyma (liquorice) .	34·35
Water . . .	27·55
Total . . .	100·00

PEREIRA.

ORANGE (*Juice*).

Citric acid,
Malic acid,
Mucilage,
Albumen,
Sugar,
Citrate of lime,
Water.

MELON (*Flesh*).

Crystallisable sugar	1·5
Pectic acid	traces
Uncrystallisable sugar, vegetable albumen, mucilage, free acid, suponifiable fat, nitrogenous matter, colouring matter, aromatic matter, starch, lignine, salts, water . .	98·5
Total . . .	100·0

Ibid.

LEMON (*Juice*).

Citric acid,
Malic acid,
Gum,
Bitter extractive,
Water.

RED CURRANT (*Juice*).

Citric acid,
Malic acid,
Sugar,
Vegetable jelly,
Gum,
Extractive.   PEREIRA.

BLACK CURRANT.

" Constituents similar to those of the red currants, with the addition of a peculiar volatile principle, and a violet colouring matter."

GOOSEBERRIES.

	Unripe.	*Ripe.*
Nitrogenous matter	1·07	0·86
Colouring matter	0·03	0·00
Lignine and seeds	8·45	8·01
Gum (pectine ?)	1·36	0·78
Sugar	0·52	6·24
Malic acid	1·80	2·41
Citric acid	0·12	0·31
Lime	0·24	0·29
Water	86·41	81·10
Total	100·00	100·00

Ibid.

MULBERRIES.

Colouring matter,	Sugar,
Pectine,	Woody fibre,
Bitartrate of potash,	Water.

PINEAPPLE (*Juice*).

Peculiar aroma,	Citric acid,
Sugar,	Tartaric acid,
Gum,	Water.
Malic acid,	

RASPBERRY.

Volatile oil,

Citric acid,

Malic acid,

Crystallisable fermentable sugar,

Red colouring matter,

Mucus,

Woody fibre,

Pectine,

Ashes containing carbonate, phosphate, and muriate of potash, carbonate and phosphate of lime and magnesia ; silica and oxide of iron.

STRAWBERRY.

Peculiar volatile aroma,

Sugar,

Mucilage,

Pectine,

Citric and malic acids, equal parts,

Woody fibre,

Pericarp, and water.

APRICOT.

	Unripe.	Ripe.
Nitrogenous matter .	0·76	0·17
Colouring matter .	0·04	0·10
Lignine . .	3·61	1·86
Gum (pectine ?) .	4·10	5·12
Sugar . .	traces	16·48
Malic acid .	2·10	1·83
Lime, very small quantity .	...	...
Water . .	89·39	74·44
Total .	100·00	100·00

PEREIRA.

GREENGAGE.

	Unripe.	Ripe.
Nitrogenous matter .	0·45	0·28
Colouring matter .	0·03	0·08
Lignine . .	1·26	1·11
Gum (pectine ?) .	5·53	2·06
Sugar . .	17·71	24·81
Malic acid .	0·45	0·56
Lime . .	trace	trace
Water . .	74·57	71·10
Total .	100·00	100·00

Ibid.

In the analyses of the apricot, greengage, peach, and cherry, Dr. Pereira has omitted pectine, which is contained in most fruits, he remarks : " Pectine, or vegetable jelly, is here omitted, but is also contained in currants (red, white, and black), apples (both sweet

and sour), pears, quinces, strawberries, bilberries,
mulberries, cherries, love-apples, oranges, lemons,
quava, tamarind, also in the Jerusalem artichoke and
onion, in the carrot, turnip, celery, beet, etc."

PEACH.

	Unripe.	Ripe.
Nitrogenous matter .	0·41	0·93
Colouring matter .	0·27	0·00
Lignine . .	3·01	1·21
Gum (pectine ?) .	4·22	4·85
Sugar . .	0·63	11·61
Malic acid . .	1·07	1·10
Lime . .	0·08	0·06
Water . .	90·31	80·24
Total .	100·00	100·00

PEREIRA.

CHERRY.

	Unripe.	Ripe.
Nitrogenous matter .	0·20	0·57
Colouring matter .	0·05	0·00
Lignine . .	2·44	1·12
Gum (pectine ?) .	6·01	3·23
Sugar . .	1·12	18·12
Malic acid . .	1·75	2·01
Lime . .	0·14	0·10
Water . .	88·29	74·85
Total .	100·00	100·00

Ibid.

PEARS (*Jargonelle*).

	Unripe.	Ripe.	Rotten.
Nitrogenous matter . .	0·08	0·21	0·301
Colouring matter . .	0·08	0·01	0·000
Resin, soluble in acohol .	0·00	0·00	0·058
Lignine . . .	3·80	2·19	2·534
Gum (pectine ?) . .	3·17	2·07	3·400
Sugar . . .	6·45	11·52	11·417
Malic acid . . .	0·11	0·08	0·786
Lime . . .	0·03	0·04	traces
Water . . .	86·28	83·88	81·500
Total . .	100·00	100·00	99·996

APPLES (*Average composition*).

Nitrogenous matter . . .	0·44
Colouring matter . . .	0·10
Lignine . . .	1·40
Gum . . .	3·45
Sugar . . .	16·50
Malic acid . . .	1·10
Lime . . .	0·01
Water . . .	77·00
Total . .	100·00

ANIMAL FOOD.

100 parts of muscle or lean of

	Water.	Albumen or fibrine.	Gelatine.
Beef contains	74	20	6
Veal ,,	75	19	6

100 parts of muscle or lean of

	Water.	Albumen or fibrine.	Gelatine.
Mutton contains	71	22	7
Pork ,,	76	19	5
Chicken ,,	73	20	7
Codfish ,,	79	14	7
Haddock ,,	82	13	5
Sole ,,	79	15	6

BRANDE.

Composition per cent. of carcases, excluding head and feet :

Animals as fattened for the butcher.	Mineral matter.	Dry nitrogenous substance.	Fat.	Total dry substance.	Water.
Calf	4·5	16·5	16·5	37·5	62·5
Bullock	5·0	15·0	30·0	50·0	50·0
Lamb	3·5	11·0	35·0	49·5	50·5
Sheep	3·5	12·5	40·0	56·0	44·0
Pig	1·5	10·0	50·0	61·5	38·5

Composition, in 100 parts :

	Mineral matter.	Gelatin.	Fibrine, or albumen.	Fat.	Water.
Veal	4·5	7·5	9·0	16·5	62·5
Beef	5·0	7·0	8·0	30·0	50·0
Mutton	3·5	7·0	5·5	40·0	44·0
Pork	1·5	5·5	4·5	50·0	38·5

The following analysis by De Bibra gives a proximate idea of the *proportions* of alkaline and earthy salts in muscle :

Muscles dried at 100° C.	Percentage of ashes in Muscles	Alkaline Phosphate.	Phosphate of lime.	Sea-Salt.	Sulphate of Soda.
Hare	4·48	79·80	15·10	4·20	0·90
Roebuck	4·68	72·00	20·60	1·00	...
Ox	7·71	76·80	16·40	6·50	...
Calf	...	89·80	10·20	...	...
Fowl	5·51	84·72	13·89	1·39	...
Wild-duck	4·48	84·00	14·80	1·20	...
Perch	7·08	54·39	44·34	1·27	...
Carp	6·10	44·19	42·20	1·31	12·30

CHEESE (*Cheddar*).

Water	36·0
Curd, caseine, or cheesy matter .	29·0
Fatty matter, or butter .	30·5
Ashes (bone material) .	6·5
Total . . .	102·0

CHEESE (*Skim-milk*).

Water	44·0
Curd, caseine, or cheesy matter .	45·0
Fatty matter, or butter .	6·0
Ashes . . .	5·0
Total . .	100·0

SIBSON.

MILK (*Cow's*).

Water	.	.	. 86·0
Caseine	.	.	. 5·0
Butter	.	.	. 3·5
Sugar of milk	.	.	. 4·5
Salts	.	.	. 1·0
Total	.	.	. 100·0

MILK (*Ass's*).

Water	.	.	. 90·0
Caseine	.	.	. 2·0
Butter	.	.	. 1·5
Sugar of milk	.	.	. 6·0
Salts	.	.	. 0·5
Total	.	.	. 100·0

According to Berzelius, milk contains :

Water	.	.	.	.	. 928·75
Curd, with a little cream		.	.	.	28·00
Sugar of milk	.	.	.	.	35·00
Muriate of potash	.	.	.	.	1·70
Phosphate of potash	.	.	.	.	0·25
Lactic acid and acetate of potash, with a trace					
of lactate of iron .	.	.	.	.	6·00
Earthy phosphates	.	.	.	.	0·30
Total	.	.	.	.	1000·00

MILK (*Human*).

Water	89·5
Caseine	3·0
Butter	3·0
Sugar of milk	4·0
Salts	0·5
Total	**100·0**

Earthy matter, obtained by incineration of 1,000 parts of cow's milk. Two instances :

	I.	II.
Phosphate of lime	2·31	3·44
Phosphate of magnesia	0·42	0·64
Phosphate of peroxide of iron	0·07	0·07
Total	**2·80**	**4·15**

HAIDLEN.

The total *ash* in these instances was 4·90 and 6·77 respectively; the earthy matter, therefore, amounted to more than half.

The flesh of most *fish* contains from 1·2 to 1·4 per cent. of salts, a less average than most animal foods.

COMPOSITION OF THE OYSTER.—PASQUIER.

Flesh.	*Liquor, or Water.*
Fibrin	Osmazome
Albumen	Albumen
Gelatin ⎱ 12·6	Chloride of sodium
Osmazome	Sulphate of lime
Mucus ⎰	Sulphate of magnesia
Water 87·4	Chloride of magnesia.
	Water.
Total 100·0	

" By incineration, the organic matters yield 1·84 of a white ash, containing phosphate of lime, and the same salts as the liquor contains."

NUTRITIVE VALUE OF FOODS.— LETHEBY.

Proportion of Salts to nitrogenous constituents. (C. DE L. E.)	Substances, 100 parts.	Water	Albumen, Fibrin, etc.	Starch, Sugar, etc.	Fat.	Salts.
1 in 17·5	Human milk	89	3·5	4·2	3·0	0·2
1 in 6·4	Cow's milk	86	4·5	5·0	4·1	0·7
,,	Skimmed milk	87	4·5	5·0	2·7	0·7
,,	Butter-milk	87	4·5	5·0	0·5	0·7
1 in 9·5	Beef and mutton	73	19·0	—	5·0	2·0
1 in 31·6	Veal	77	19·0	—	1·0	0·6
1 in 17·5	Poultry	74	21·0	—	3·0	1·2
	Bacon	20	0·8	—	70·0	1·3
1 in 6·4	Cheese (Cheddar)	36	29·0	—	30·0	4·5
1 in 9·0	Cheese (skimmed)	44	45·0	—	6·0	5·0
,,	Butter	15	—	—	83·0	2·0
1 in 9·3	Eggs	74	14·0	—	10·5	1·5
1 in 12·5	White of egg	78	20·0	—	—	1·6
1 in 12·3	Yolk of egg	52	16·0	—	30·0	1·3
1 in 15·8	White fish	79	19·0	—	1·0	1·2
1 in 12·1	Salmon	78	17·0	—	4·0	1·4
1 in 7·6	Eel	80	10·0	—	8·0	1·3
1 in 6·4	Wheat flour	15	11·0	70·0	2·0	1·7
1 in ·5	Barley-meal	15	10·0	70·0	2·4	2·0
1 in ·4	Oat-meal	15	12·0	62·0	6·0	3·0
1 in ·5	Rye-meal	15	9·0	66·0	2·0	1·8
1 in 5·2	Indian-meal	14	9·0	65·0	8·0	1·7
1 in 2·3	Rice	14	7·0	76·0	0·3	0·3
1 in 6·3	Haricot	19	23·0	45·0	3·0	3·6
1 in 7·3	Pease	13	22·0	58·0	2·0	3·0
1 in 6·6	Beans	14	24·0	44·0	1·4	3·6
1 in 12·6	Lentils	14	29·0	44·0	1·5	2·3
1 in 3·9	Wheat-bread	44	9·0	49·0	1·0	2·3
1 in 3·5	Rye-bread	48	5·0	46·0	1·0	1·4
1 in 2·8	Potatoes	74	2·0	23·0	0·2	0·7
1 in 2·8	Green vegetables	86	2·0	4·0	0·5	0·7
	Arrow-root	18	—	82·0	—	—

CHAPTER III.—(*continued*).

From the foregoing analyses we see that fruits, as distinct from vegetables, have the least amount of earthy salts ; most of them contain a large quantity of water, but that water in itself is of the purest kind—a distilled water of nature, and has in solution vegetable albumen.

We also notice that they are to a great extent free from the *oxidised* albumens—glutinous and fibrinous substances, and many of them contain *acids*—citric, tartaric, malic, etc.—which when taken into the system act directly upon the blood, by increasing its solubility, by thinning it; the process of circulation is more easily carried on, and the blood flows more easily in the capillaries (which become lessened in calibre as age advances) than it would if of a thicker nature. By this means the blood flows easily in vessels which have been perhaps for years lost to the passage of a thicker fluid. Further, these acids *lower* the temperature of the body, therefore the process of wasting, combustion, or oxidation, which increases in ratio to the temperature of the body, as indicated by the thermometer.

These acids are chiefly compounds of carbon, hydrogen, and oxygen ; they differ from the mineral acids in being burnt up in the system, and are therefore not traceable to the secretions and excretions.

Some fruits contain tannic acid, which acts beneficially on the system, by tanning or hardening the albuminous and gelatinous structures—rendering them more leather-like, and less susceptible to the corroding action of atmospheric oxygen, therefore less liable to waste or decay.

Most fruits contain, combined with the above mentioned acids, *alkalies*, generally potash, which, on the combustion of the acids (citric, tartaric, etc.), are left in solution in the blood.

Alkalies increase the solubility of albumen and fibrin, and therefore tend to prevent undue fibrinous accumulation in or around the smaller bloodvessels.

Fruits contain very little nitrogen, as compared with the so-called nitrogenous or highly-nourishing foods. Many physiologists and physiological chemists have calculated the amount of nitrogen they think it necessary to sustain life. This amount was dictated to them by experiments : these experiments were to find the amount *excreted* by the system.

It is a simple fact that the greater the quantity of nitrogen taken into the system, the greater is the amount eliminated; and it is very often observed in overfed people, that organs whose purpose is to eliminate nitrogenous products are unable to carry off any great excess, and free nitrogen is often eliminated by the skin.

Therefore this process of inquiry cannot possibly give a correct result.

A proper estimate of the amount of nitrogen required to sustain life can only be obtained by *direct* experiments—that is, living for a time on one class of food, then on another, and calculating the amount taken into the system, and the amount excreted, and during the time the experiments are carried on to weigh the body in order to ascertain loss or gain.* By this means a proximate amount required to keep the body in equilibrio may be obtained.

By experiments on ourselves, on friends, and on natives of tropical regions, we find a comparatively small quantity of nitrogen necessary to sustain life, in good bodily health—in fact, fruits, taken as a class, contain sufficient nitrogen to sustain human life.†

Many authors state that five or six ounces of gum† (which contains carbon, hydrogen, oxygen, and little or no nitrogen), in the twenty-four hours, is sufficient to sustain life.

Adanson states that the nomadic Moors have scarcely any other food than gum-senegal, and Hasselquist asserts, that a caravan of Abyssinians, consisting of 1000 persons, subsisted for two months on gum-arabic alone.

Humboldt relates that the natives on the coast of Caraccas prefer sugar‡ to animal food, and we have ourselves observed on the West Coast of Africa many tribes who subsist upon foods which contain comparatively little nitrogen.

Plants absorb most of their *nitrogen* from the *air*. If a vegetable be supplied with ammonia (a compound of nitrogen and hydrogen), those parts of it which

---

* The weight of the body is not necessarily a criterion of the value of food, because the weight may not alter, but water increase, and albumen and fat diminish in the system.

† The amount of nitrogen *excreted* is often greater than the amount *taken into* the system *as food and drink*.

‡ *Impure* gum and *raw* sugar contain small quantities of nitrogen.

6

would, without it, be deposited as starch (which contains no nitrogen) become *gluten*, a substance which contains the same elements as albumen (carbon, hydrogen, oxygen, and nitrogen).

It has been argued that fruits will not sustain life because they do not contain sufficient nitrogen ; this argument is founded upon a *theory* which is demonstrably incorrect, and it is an ascertained *fact* that fruits alone will support life in good bodily health.

The experiments of Macaire and Marcet prove that the blood contains more nitrogen than chyle.*

As the blood is formed from the chyle, the excess of nitrogen found in the blood must have another source than from the intestines, which source can only be the lungs or the skin, both of which are exposed to the atmosphere.

Sir Humphry Davy states, that in his experiments the absorption of nitrogen took place to the extent of 2246 grains in the twenty-four hours.

When nitrogen comes in contact with hydrogen in a nascent state in an enclosed space, the two unite and form ammonia. Hydrogen is developed in the intestines and in the capillaries, therefore throughout the system wherever there is waste of tissue. It is possible that either ammonia, coming in contact with amylaceous substances destitute of nitrogen, or that these bodies, containing carbon, hydrogen, and oxygen,

---

* This can be only *partially* accounted for in the lacteals ; after passing through the mesenteric glands, and receiving the lymph from the spleen, fat is decreased, fibrin increased, in their contents.

may unite directly with free nitrogen—the combination resulting in albumen or protein.

Now, fruits will sustain life, and all fruits contain carbon, hydrogen, and oxygen, and most of them a small quantity of nitrogen ; and if these fruits which will sustain life do not contain sufficient nitrogen, may not man, who breathes and is in contact with an atmosphere (four-fifths of which are nitrogen), by means of his lungs, the surface of which is supposed to be more than twenty times that of the whole body, absorb the necessary nitrogen directly from the atmosphere ?

From careful observation on the diet of natives in tropical regions, and from direct experiments in England, we may state that this is positively the case.

This is often observed in the herbivora : their *natural* food contains little nitrogen, still it is found in their flesh to about the same extent as in the carnivora. Further, the carnivora live on food rich in nitrogen—yet one is as well nourished as the other.

Speaking of the *ancients*, Hesiod, the Greek poet, says : " The uncultivated fields afforded them their *fruits*, and supplied their bountiful and unenvied repast."

Porphyry, a Platonic philosopher of the third century, a man of great talent and learning, says : " The ancient Greeks lived entirely upon the *fruits* of the earth."

Lucretius,* on the same subject, says :

* Creech's translation.

" Soft acorns were their first and chiefest food,
 And those red apples that adorn the wood.
 The nerves that joined their limbs were firm and strong ;
 Their life was healthy, and their age was long. . . .
 Returning years still saw them in their prime ;
 They wearied e'en the wings of measuring Time :
 No colds, nor heats, no strong diseases wait,
 And tell sad news of coming hasty fate :
 Nature not yet grew weak, not yet began
 To shrink into an inch the largest span."

Wherever we find animal life throughout nature, we find its manifestation in development, growth, and nutrition depending upon the presence of albumen. The first visible state of an organised being is albumen; it is built up from albumen; its harder structures are caused by the oxidation of albumen; its food is albumen, which may (with the exception of what little may be formed* in the system) always be traced to, and was originally vegetable albumen; if that food be vegetable food, this substance comes directly from the vegetable : if it be animal food, it comes originally from the vegetable through the medium of the animal.

" The continuance of life is indissolubly connected with its presence in the blood—that is, in the nutrient fluid; only those substances are in a strict sense nutritious articles of food which contain either albumen, or a substance capable of being converted into albumen."—LIEBIG.

It *is* one of *nature's laws*, and a very simple one, that we are built up from what originally was vege-

Formed in the system by the union of amylaceous substances with nitrogen.

table albumen; and with the exception of the alkaline and earthy salts, every structure and organ in our bodies was developed from and is nourished by albumen. It *was* one of the laws of Eden that man should eat albumen—vegetable albumen—in its purest form, as it exists in fruits.

There is, therefore, a simplicity, a reason, a wonderful philosophy in the first command given to man.

Man may live entirely upon fruits, in better health than the majority of mankind now enjoy. Good, sound, ripe fruits are never a cause of disease, but the vegetable acids, as we have before stated, *lower* the temperature of the body, decrease the process of combustion or oxidation—therefore the waste of the system—less sleep* is required, activity is increased, fatigue or thirst hardly experienced : still the body is well nourished, and as a comparatively small quantity of earthy salts are taken into the system, the *cause* of " old age" is in some degree removed, the *effect* is delayed, and life is prolonged to a period far beyond our " threescore years and ten."

Animal flesh, taken as a class, contains, next to fruits, the least amount of earthy salts. The amount depends, *firstly*, upon the quantity contained in the food of the animal; *secondly*, upon the duration of time the animal has eaten such food—that is, its age. Younger

---

° On one occasion, when living for five days entirely upon *oranges*, our temperature was lessened, still we felt a pleasant glow throughout the system ; but to other individuals we felt cold, animal heat is therefore only *relative ;* we further found that only three or four hours' sleep was required in the twenty-four hours.

animals of every class contain a less amount of earthy salts in their flesh than older ones; thus veal, in the analyses generally given, contains only about one-fourth the amount of earthy salts found in an equal weight of the flesh of an adult animal, and it further contains from 12 to 15 per cent. more phosphoric acid than is necessary for the formation of salts.

From this we see that the younger the animal, the less ossifying matter does its flesh contain; we should, therefore, select either growing animals or those just arrived at maturity, in preference to older animals, as a diet.

Amongst animal flesh we include *fish*. Those which have fins and scales contain, on an average, a percentage less salts (about ·7) than animal flesh, and are therefore, to a certain extent, better adapted as a diet to longevity than butchers' meat. Fish also contains phosphorus; this is especially marked in most shell-fish, which, however, contain more earthy matter than fish with fins and scales.

The flesh of poultry and game (if young) contains less earthy salts than beef or mutton.

Animal flesh without fat will support life; gelatine or jelly, although containing nearly as much nitrogen as muscular fibre, will not: the reason is that digestion is incapable of converting it into albumen. Dogs fed on gelatine alone soon died, but they have lived many months on pure albuminous matter.

" The true unsophisticated American Indians near the sources of the Missouri, during the winter months, are reported to subsist entirely upon dried buffalo flesh—not the fat portions, but the muscular part. . . .

During their subsistence on dried *pemmican*, they are
described by travellers, who were intimate with their
habits of life, as never tasting even the most minute
portions of any vegetable whatever, or partaking of
any other variety of food. These facts, then, tend to
show that *albuminous* tissue is of *itself* capable of sus-
taining life."—DR. THOMPSON.

In other articles of animal food we have *milk*, un-
skimmed, skimmed, and butter-milk; they all contain
about ·7 per cent. of salts; but the latter contains a
large quantity of lactic acid, which has a great
tendency to prevent the accumulation of earthy matter
in the system.

Cheese contains salts in about the same proportion
as milk deprived of its water. It seems by its analysis
to have a large quantity of salts (nearly 5 per cent.),
but they exist in ratio to its highly nourishing properties.

Butter is composed of fat, and contains about 2 per
cent. of salts. It is not a fat either formed or altered
in the animal economy. It may be artificially produced from grass, and may therefore be termed the
"fat of the land."

Eggs contain 1·5 per cent. of salts (·5 per cent. less
than beef and mutton).

We will now briefly consider the *vegetable roots*.
The potato contains ·9 per cent. of salts, 1·4 of albuminous matter, and 15·5 of starch; it contains sugar,
a small quantity of fat, and a small proportion of free
citric acid.

The onion is very nutritious, and it contains small
quantities of phosphate of lime, but there is an *excess*

of phosphoric acid; also mucilage, and a substance analogous to gluten.

Most other *roots* contain a large quantity of water, and, in proportion to their nutrient properties, a large quantity of fibrous and earthy matter. Most other *vegetables* have about the same nourishing properties as the potato, about the same amount of earthy salts,* but contain more water and less starch. The cucumber and fungi are exceptions, and are similar to fruit.

We now come to the *cereals,* in which we will include the leguminous seeds. The amount of earthy salts they contain depends upon the amount contained in the soil, or in substances used as manure.

The cereals constitute the basis of man's food; they mostly contain large quantities of mineral matter,† and as a class are the worst adapted as a food for man,

---

° The amount of earthy salts they contain depends entirely upon the soil in which they are grown. If we take one dram of cress-seed, incinerate it, and weigh the amount of salts it contains; and if we take another dram of the same seed, and place it on flannel (which has been soaked for some weeks in distilled water to free it from soluble salts) in a vessel, and fill the vessel with distilled water, to a level with the flannel, the seeds will grow and become plants, almost as perfect as if grown in soil; if we then dry and incinerate these plants, they are found to contain exactly the same amount of salts as that existing in the seed from which they grew. The salts previously contained in the seeds have been, by the process of growth, distributed in the substance of the plants.

† " The system obtains its supply of *earthy* substances from both animal and vegetable foods. *Corn, potatoes, milk,* and the *flesh* and *blood* of animals *furnish* us with *more than the wants of the system require.*"—DR. PEREIRA.

in regard to a long life. Man's so-called "staff of life" is, to a great extent, the cause of his premature death.

"Notwithstanding that bread is denominated the *staff of life,* alone it does *not* appear to be *capable* of supporting *prolonged human existence.* Boussingault came to this conclusion from observing the small quantity of nitrogen which it contains; and the Reports of the Inspectors of Prisons, on the effect of a diet of bread and water, favour this opinion."— PEREIRA.

Magendie fed a dog exclusively on fine wheaten bread—it died in forty days; whilst another dog, fed on black bread (brown bread—flour with the bran), lived without any disturbance in good health.

The nutrient part of wheat is chiefly gluten. *Bran is rich in gluten, and should therefore not be removed.*

Leguminous seeds (peas, beans, etc.) are supposed to be less nutritive than the cereals, although the former contain more nitrogen than the latter. This Liebig attributes to a deficiency of *earthy phosphates,* which, however, could not be the reason, as Broconnot gives *peas* as containing 9·26 grains per ounce of earthy phosphates. This is nearly twice the quantity found in wheat, and more than twenty times the amount in an equal weight of beef.

Phosphoric acid and the alkalies have both of them remarkable properties, and play an important part in the growth and nutrition of plants and animals.

This cannot be said of the *earthy* salts. They develop the bones of animals, but when this is accom-

plished they accumulate and cause the ossification of
" old age"—even " natural death."

We should, therefore, after we arrive at maturity,
avoid as much as possible *earthy* salts in our food.

Many interesting and well-conducted experiments of
agricultural chemists agree, and give the following
facts :

1. Vegetables and cereals grown in soil containing
a small percentage of *earthy* salts, contain a less
amount than those grown in soil rich in earthy salts.

2. The greater the quantity of earthy salts contained
in the food on which an animal subsists, the greater is
the amount found in the secretions and excretious, and
the greater is the amount found in the *flesh* of the
animal.

3. The less the amount of earthy salts in the food,
the less the amount found in the secretions and excretions, and the less the amount in the flesh.   The
result of these experiments thus favours in the abstract
what we adopt in the principle.

From these facts it is clear, that in growing cereals
and vegetables directly for the consumption of man,
or indirectly for the food of animals on which he partly
subsists, *Lime or any of its compounds should not be
used as a manure*.   Alkalies do not accumulate in the
system, there is, therefore, no objection to their use.

We therefore see that the different kinds of food, in
regard to longevity, have the following order : fruits,
fish, animal food (flesh, eggs, etc.), vegetables, cereals.

In the same order do we trace the age of man by
his diet.   It is written that man in the first ages lived
for a period which to us seems incredible ; but in the

present generation the average time of life is so short, that a man at eighty or ninety years is truly a modern "patriarch." Man's first and ordained diet was fruits; he then eat animal food, which was subsequently permitted to him; after this he gained a knowledge of agriculture—he grew vegetables and cereals; and not content with this, during the last few years, he has learned to add lime artificially to them—to shrink and lessen an already shortened existence.

In nature a curious yet simple phenomenon is often observed—a *rise* and *fall*. If perpetual, it alternates and becomes a fall and rise. We notice it in the sun, in gravity, in fluctuation, in the tides, and even in the rise and fall of empires.

Man has degenerated—this degeneration is due solely to his diet. He has *fallen;* but we hope that he has *risen* to the highest point in the art of shortening his days, and that in the present generation he will commence to gradually *fall* back on his original and ordained diet. Since the creation, the days of man's existence have been little by little decreasing— it has been a gradual *fall;* but both science and religion tell us that he must *rise* again, that his life on earth must be prolonged. This can only be accomplished by a gradual alteration in his diet.

Let us imagine a man, who is a great smoker, suddenly deprived of tobacco. What would be his feelings?

Let us picture to ourselves a man, enjoying all the luxuries and enjoyments of modern life, suddenly deprived of them. What would be his feelings? They would both be for a time wretched and miserable.

It is not our purpose to dictate a course which would have a similar result. Our purpose is by pointing out a method of gradually altering diet, to endeavour to improve and benefit humanity, and to lengthen the days and increase the happiness of man.

"Nature is frugal, and her wants are few." Man in the savage state is generally healthy, in the *civilised* state he is generally unhealthy; and, as Dr. Thompson says, "There is no doubt that a simple diet is more fitted to accelerate health than unnatural and stimulating foods." It is not necessary that man should return to the savage state in order that he should enjoy health, nor does it follow that because man in his wild state is healthy, civilised man should be diseased; particularly when he awakens to the fact that diet is the great cause of his sufferings, and that the antidote rests to a great extent with himself—that the nearer he approaches to his original diet, the more healthy will he be.

"We cannot expect a nation to bound and stride into perfection at once. It was only by slow painful efforts that a nation worked out its redemption from darkness and ignorance."—LORD ROSEBERY.

It would be a difficult task, and a great tax on the system, for a man who lives on an ordinary mixed diet to suddenly change it. He must do this gradually; and in direct ratio as he does this will the tendency to disease decrease, and the prospect of long life increase.

If we look at the ordinary articles of diet, we notice to a great extent the following principle: that the more nitrogenous substances—*direct* nourishment—a food contains, the more earthy salts are there found in it; and the less the nourishment, the less the amount of earthy salts in the food.

It is a well-known fact that the more nitrogenous substances a food contains, the less is the amount required to nourish the body; and inversely, the less the amount of these substances, the greater is the amount required to sustain life. If we take cheese and rice as an example, the former contains far more nitrogen, also far more earthy salts than the latter. But a small quantity of cheese will support life, whilst in order to live on rice, a man must eat a large quantity; so that one man whilst eating a small quantity of cheese, rich in nitrogen and earthy salts, another, living on rice, must eat a proportionately large quantity; and in the end both consume about the same amount of nitrogenous substances, and about the same amount of earthy salts. Fruits are the great exception to this rule, but others are observed, as for instance: one man subsists on bread, another, we will say, on mutton. In order to obtain the same nourishment in both cases, the bread-eater would have to eat more than twice the quantity consumed by the other, and he would further take into his system two and a half times more earthy salts than the flesh-eater. Lentils are another exception; and in proportion to their nourishing properties, they contain only one-third the amount of earthy salts as compared with bread.

Before selecting a diet, or giving any rules thereon, a word on the question of quantity is requisite. One authority says "that a full-grown man of average weight (140 to 150 lbs.), and height (5ft. 7in.), requires *one-twentieth* part of his weight in food during the twenty-four hours; that is, *seven or seven and a half pounds* of food, including solids and liquids, *one to one and a half pound* (sixteen to twenty-four ounces) being *solids*, the rest water.

Another authority says *eight pounds of food* are required daily, *two pounds* of which must be *solid*, the remaining *six pounds liquid*.

Now these results are arrived at by *indirect* experiment, determining the waste; and we have before pointed out that this principle of inquiry cannot possibly give a correct result, because the greater the amount of food and drink a man takes into his system, the greater will be the amount of solids, liquids, and gases excreted and eliminated by the body. *Direct* experiment only will give us a correct result, and we have positive evidence to show that little more than half the above quantities of solids are necessary to keep the body *in equilibrio*—to sustain life.

" It may with truth be asserted that the greater part of mankind eat more than is necessary; and by being crammed and over-fed in infancy, we are deprived of that natural sensation which ought to tell us when we have enough."—HUFELAND.

A good instance of this is seen in the well-known case of Louis Cornaro, who, " till the fortieth year of his age, had led a life of dissipation . . . and was so far reduced that his physician assured him he could not live above two months; that all medicines would be useless, and that the only thing which could be recommended for him was a *spare diet.* Having followed this advice, he found, after some days, he was much better; and at the end of a few years his health was not only perfectly re-established, but he became sounder than ever he had been before. . . . For *sixty whole years* he took no more than *twelve ounces of food*, everything included, and *thirteen ounces of drink*, daily . . . When he was eighty years of age, his friends prevailed upon him to make a little addition to his food . . .; he gave way to their request, and raised his food to fourteen, and his drink to sixteen ounces. ' Scarcely,' says he, ' had I continued this mode of living ten days, when I began, instead of being cheerful and lively as before, to become uneasy and dejected, a burden to myself and to others. . . . But by the blessing of God, and my *former regimen*, I recovered; and now, in my eighty-third year, I enjoy a happy state of body and mind. I can climb steep hills . . . and I am a stranger to those peevish and morose humours which fall so often to the lot of old age.' In this happy disposition he attained his hundredth year."—HUFELAND.

"A cheerful and a good heart will have a care for his meat and diet." Gluttony is truly a sin, not legally punishable, but revengeful in itself on the individual; it is the cause of a distinct debility from loss of nerve-power in digesting excess of food, and the sufferer, although gormandising and eating ravenously, becomes thinner and thinner, weaker and weaker, and in his efforts to nourish his pining frame he creeps nearer and nearer to the jaws of *premature death*.

Obesity is sometimes caused by over-eating, but this is not always the case, for we see many corpulent persons who are very small eaters. Want of proper exercise is the commonest cause.

Many diseases have excessive eating solely as a cause. Remove the cause, the effect cannot follow. A state of bodily equilibrium, which we will designate by the word *health*, is the result of a conformity to the laws of nature ; apart from this, there can only be the conditions *plus* and *minus*—excess or deficiency ; and where either of these diverge to any considerable extent, we have *disease*.

Although thoroughly acquainted with the effects of deficient food, on inquiry we are bound to come to the conclusion that many cases of starvation—the results of famine or insufficient nourishment—are often due to the *quality*, more than the *quantity*, of food.

Dr. Aitken quotes the following diet of labourers under the old "truck system," which was often the cause of outbreaks of *scurvy* : "His daily diet consisted of *one pennyworth of bread, with tea, but no milk, in the morning ; no dinner ; and one pennyworth of bread, with tea, and no milk, in the evening.* After existing *three months* on this diet, the disease broke out." What else could be expected ? Bread *alone* is not a proper diet for man. Had he added to it but a small quantity of his original, ordained, and best adapted diet—fruits, experience tells us he would not have been afflicted.

White bread and gelatin are popularly supposed to be very nutritious. Now a man may feed an animal on bread and gelatin, and under the erroneous impression he is feeding the animal well, give it pounds a day, but many experiments tell us that in time the animal will die of starvation—deficiency of *proper* nourishing food.

Did man know the *quality* of foods, had he the power of discriminating why he should eat this and avoid that, he would be able to live on far less than he at present does, and he would further be less subject to disease. For this reason we think that it is requisite that every child should be taught at school, and should be made acquainted with, the elements of himself and the food by which his body is nourished, in the full impression that his well-being depends more upon this knowledge than a study of the dead languages and theoretical sciences.

This reminds us that as yet we have not mentioned childhood, but as our remarks are chiefly confined to those arrived at maturity, a lengthy discourse on the subject is unnecessary. A few words, however, may not be out of place. In the word childhood we will include that period of life which commences in infancy (at birth), and extends to early adult age (maturity). We therefore speak of that time of life during which the development of the different organs and textures is proceeding, and their functions becoming more perfect; during which, also, the mental manifestations, intellectual, moral, and emotional, develop and gain strength. In infancy, or commencing childhood, the functions are chiefly vegetative, and the movements, to a great extent, automatic, and during this period all the organs, particularly the osseous, nervous, and locomotary systems, are in a state of development. During this period the infant's food is *milk*.

In infancy, nourishment is' required for the growth of the soft structures—*albumen* will answer this purpose ; also for the hard structures, cartilage and bone

7

—*chondrine* and the salts contained in milk will do all that is necessary.

The nutrient part of milk is chiefly its *caseine,* and if to the formula of caseine be added ten eqs. of oxygen, we obtain a formula which contains exactly the same elements as the albumen of blood and chondrine.

The formulæ as given by Liebig are :

	Sulphur. Eqs.	Nitrogen. Eqs.	Carbon. Eqs.	Hydrogen. Eqs.	Oxygen. Eqs.
The formula of *chondrine* is .	—	9	72	59	32
Add the formula of *albumen* of blood . .	2	27	216	169	68
Total .	2	36	288	228	100
Together = the formula of *caseine* (of milk)	2	36	288	228	90
+ 10 eqs. of oxygen .	—	—	—	—	10

The oxygen the child readily gets from the atmosphere by the process of respiration, and if to this we add the salts, alkaline and earthy, contained in milk, we find albumen as the chief constituent of its blood —the developing and nutrient fluid of every organ and structure; chondrine and salts, to develop its cartilages and bones. Thus in milk nature supplies childhood with all its wants, and for this reason milk is a food better fitted to childhood than adult life.

It is a well-known fact that children brought up on

human milk are healthier and more robust than children fed on cow's milk. The reason is obvious. The salts in *human milk* exist in ratio to its nourishing properties, as one part of salts to seventeen and a half parts of nitrogenous matter; in *cow's* milk, as one part of salts to six and one-third parts of the same nourishing substances. Therefore, in round numbers, the nutrient part of cow's milk contains nearly three times the amount of salts as compared with human milk. The proportions of alkaline and earthy salts are proximately the same in the ashes of both, so that one ounce of caseine taken from cow's milk contains nearly three times the amount of *earthy* salts found in an equal weight of caseine from human milk.

A human being takes four or five times longer to mature than a cow; the latter therefore grows more quickly, and its bones ossify in a less period of time than the former, whose organs are more gradual in their development and growth—whose bones should take a longer time to ossify, and therefore nature gives a food which contains less *earthy* matter. If we do not follow nature's laws, some bad result must follow, and one-half of our strumous children, who, besides their milk, are, as a rule, fed on bread and other farinaceous foods—most of them rich in earthy compounds—are for their age, in years and months, bodily older than healthy and robust children of the same age.

Rickets and mollities ossium are in themselves diseases, not necessarily caused by a deficiency of earthy salts in the food, but by a lack in the system of power to assimilate them.

We can stunt the growth of the lower animals by

7—2

giving them an excess of earthy matter ; we can ossify them, make them permanently old, and shorten their days, by the same. In human beings we need not look further than the Cretins found in the valleys of the Alps, Pyrenees, and other regions. Although cretinism has two * distinct causes, the first and most important is that an excess of *earthy* matter—lime or magnesian lime—is taken into the system in solution in water used for drinking purposes. Hereditary it must be to children born of parents suffering from this disease, if not removed from the cause ; but sound healthy children brought into districts where cretinism exists, are, at an early age, equally subject to the disease with children born in them.

Now these beings are, in their infancy, literally prematurely ossified, the development of the bones is arrested, the height being seldom more than four and a half feet. The bones of the cranium, which in a natural state should expand to allow the brain to grow and develop, at 'an early age becomes thickened, hardened, and ossified to such an extent that expansion is impossible ; the brain, therefore, cannot develop ; it is gradually deprived of its blood-supply from below ;

---

* The other cause is an electro-magnetic action due to the peculiar *geological* formations in some districts where cretinism prevails, and which influences the excretion of earthy salts from the system. For there are many recorded cases of this disease where the afflicted persons did not use lime, or *hard* water—in fact, where the water was *soft*, the sufferers eating the same or a similar diet to persons free from the disease, but not resident in the district. Both, therefore, take into their systems about the same amount of calcareous salts, but the one *excretes* nearly the whole, the other *retains* the same.

it is encased and imprisoned by its own shield; its intellectual part cannot develop; the being is subservient to the animal portion; he becomes voracious and lascivious, and in many cases sinks in intelligence below the level of many of the brutes. The age of Cretins is short, few of them reach thirty years, and, as Clayton remarks, "that although they die early, they soon present the appearance of age." This miserable state of existence is due, to a great extent, to *premature* ossification.

It is therefore clear that infants should be fed on *human* milk; that children, during their growth, should not be fed almost entirely on foods rich in earthy salts —on a cereal or farinaceous diet; time should be given for the expansion and development of their bodies. They should, therefore, eat a mixed diet—fruits or animal food in excess of the farinaceous; and further, as use determines the shape of a limb, exercise and athletic games should be encouraged; and as the *mind* influences the character, sympathies, and welfare of man, and places him by its activity and development at the head of all animated creation, education—the fountain of intellectual manifestations, of sound principles of action and conduct, of the elegancies, accomplishments, and endearments of life—should be carried out in a manner which will be attractive to, and appreciated by, the receiver of *knowledge*; so that in decomposing the information thus acquired, and recombining it in useful and attractive forms, he may lay the foundation in learning, from the supervision and experience of the good, and upon it construct a castle of *wisdom*— but not at the expense of bodily health.

" *Knowledge* and *Wisdom*, far from being one,
   Have ofttimes no connection. *Knowledge* dwells
In heads replete with thoughts of other men ;
Wisdom in minds attentive to their own.
Knowledge, a rude unprofitable mass,
The mere materials with which *Wisdom* builds,
Till smooth'd, and squar'd, and fitted to its place,
Doth but encumber whom it seems t' enrich.
Knowledge is proud that he has learn'd so much ;
Wisdom is humble that she knows no more."

                                Cowper.

To return to the subject of *quantity* of food required to sustain life, we affirm that most men eat more than is requisite for this purpose—more than is actually good for them. Man does not require four or five meals a day ; he would be in far better health on two, or at most three, meals in the twenty-four hours.

Fruits are nutritious in themselves ; but should they not contain sufficient nitrogen to satisfy a *theoretical* appetite, we have shown that all other elements are present, and that man may absorb the deficient nitrogen from the surrounding atmosphere, the combination resulting in albumen, or protein. For this reason, together with the fact that they contain little earthy matter, fruits are man's best diet if he truly desires a long life ; but considering the difficulties attending a sudden change of diet, and the necessity of conforming to the rules and usages of society, which we do not wish to usurp (and even did we desire this, we fear society would be the victor), we are induced to put forward a few *simple* and straightforward *rules*, which are founded upon observed facts, which are not oppressive or tyrannical, which would not interfere with the avocations and callings of man, and which may be readily carried out by every one of the community for his own individual benefit, for health and long life.

As we know there are many who could not be persuaded to make any alteration in the *articles* of their diet, whilst there are others who might be influenced in this direction, we give a few rules for both these classes.

To those who are not inclined to alter the articles 'of their diet, we say :

1. Eat *moderately*, always remembering that you eat to live—to give a balance to the system.

2. Take no more than three meals a day.

3. *Avoid* eating *large quantities* of bread, pastry, and other farinaceous foods.

To those who are willing to make alterations in their diet, the same rules will apply, but with this difference :

Eat *fruits*, if possible, at every meal, and commence with them ; if the appetite is not moderately satisfied, finish with the ordinary articles of diet.

CHAPTER IV.

INSTANCES OF LONGEVITY IN MAN AND IN THE ANIMAL AND VEGETABLE KINGDOMS.

ON reviewing nearly two thousand well-authenticated cases of persons who lived more than a century, we generally find some peculiarity of diet or habits to account for their longevity; we find some were living amongst all the luxuries life could afford, others in the most abject poverty—begging their bread; some were samples of symmetry and physique, others cripples; some drank large quantities of water, others little; some were total abstainers from alcoholic drinks, others drunkards; some smoked tobacco, others did not; some lived entirely on vegetables, others to a great extent on animal foods; some led active lives, others sedentary; some worked with their brain, others with their hands; some ate only one meal a day, others four or five; some few ate large quanities of food, others a small amount; in fact we notice great divergence both in habits and diet, but in those cases where we have been able to obtain a reliable account of the diet, we find one *great cause* which accounts for the majority of cases of longevity, *moderation in the quantity of food.*

To illustrate this we append a few authenticated cases from Easton, Hufeland, Bailey, and other authors.

Judith Bannister, of Cowes, Isle of Wight, died in 1754, aged 108.

"She lived upon biscuit and *apples,* with milk and water, the last sixty years of her life."

Ann Maynard, of Finchley, died in 1756, aged 112.

" She lived with *moderation*, and took much exercise."

John Michaelstone (grandson of Thomas Parr), died in 1763, aged 127.

" He lived to the above great age by *extreme temperance.*"

Owen Carollan, of Duleck, county Meath, died in 1764, aged 127.

" By *temperance* and hard labour he attained so great an age."

Janet Anderson, of Newington, Middlesex, died in 1764, aged 102.

" Her life was *regular and moderate.*"

Elizabeth Macpherson, lived in the county of Caithness, died in 1765, aged 117.

" Her diet was *buttermilk and greens ;* she retained all her senses till within three months of her death."

Mr. Dobson, of Hatfield, farmer, died in 1766, aged 139.

" By much exercise and *temperate living* he preserved the inestimable blessing of health."

Francis Confit, of Burythorpe, near Malton, Yorkshire, died in 1767, aged 150.

" He was *very temperate in his living,* and used great exercise, which, together with occasionally eating a *raw egg,* enabled him to attain such extraordinary age."

Catherine Noon *alias* Noony, lived near the city of Tuam, in Ireland, died the same year, aged 136.

" Was *very temperate at her meals.* Her husband died aged 128."

Philip Loutier, of Shoreditch, London, a French barber, died at 105.

"He drank nothing but water, and *ate only once a day.*"

Donald M'Gregor, a farmer in the Isle of Skye, died at 117.

"*He was temperate at his meals,* and took much exercise."

Mrs. Boyce, of Guildford, Surrey, died in 1771, aged 107.

"By *temperance* she acquired constant health."

Paul Barral, of Nice, a priest, died in 1771, aged 106.

"He continued in good health by living on vegetables."

Mrs. Keithe, of Newnham, Gloucestershire, died in 1772, aged 133.

"She *lived moderately,* and retained her senses till within fourteen days of her death."

Mrs. Clum, lived near Lichfield, Staffordshire, died in 1773, aged 138.

"By frequent exercise and *temperate living* she attained so great longevity . . . . she resided in the same house 103 years."

Mary Rogers, of Penzance, Cornwall, died in 1779, aged 118.

"Lived the last sixty years on *vegetables.*"

Fluellyn Price, of Glamorgan, died the same year, aged 101.

"Possessed a great flow of spirits, attended with sound health and activity, which blessings were the result of his *abstemious manner of living.* Herb teas were his breakfast, meat plainly dressed his dinner, and *instead* of a supper he refreshed himself with smoking a pipe of tobacco."

Joseph Ekins, of Combe, Berks, labourer, died in 1780, aged 103.

"Never suffered a week's illness, and for the last forty years subsisted entirely on bread, milk and *vegetables.*"

Henry Grosvenor, of Inch, county Wexford, a gentleman of French extraction, surveyor of the coast of Blackwater, died in 1780, aged 115.

"*He was very sparing in his diet,* and used much exercise, and was an agreeable, cheerful companion at one hundred, when he married his last wife."

Val. Coleby, of Preston, near Hull, died in 1782, aged 116.

"His diet for twenty years was milk and biscuit."

Edward Drinker, of Philadelphia, died in 1782, aged 103.

"He lived on very solid food, drank tea in the afternoon, but *ate no supper.*"

Alexander Mackintosh, of Marseilles, died at 112.

"For the last ten years he lived *entirely on vegetables,* and enjoyed a good state of health till within two days of his death."

James Le Measurer, of St. Jean Pied de Port, in Navarre, died in 1784, aged 118.

"His common food for some years was *vegetables.*"

Lewis Morgan, of Llwringtdod, Radnorshire, died at 101.

" His death was occasioned by a fall . . . he lived chiefly on *vegetable diet.*"

Mr. Smith, of Dolver, Montgomeryshire, farmer, died in 1785, aged 103.

" He was never known to drink anything but *butter-milk.*"

Cardinal de Salis, Archbishop of Seville, died the same year, aged 125.

He himself observed : " I led a sober, studious, but not a lazy or sedentary life. My *diet was sparing,* though delicate; my liquors the best wines of Xeres and La Mancha, of which I never exceeded a pint at any meal, except in cold weather, when I allowed myself one-third more."

Margaret M'Carthy, of Cork, died in 1789, aged 103.

" She lived *abstemiously,* and was very regular at her *meals.*"

Anne Bannerman died the same year at Aberdeen, aged 105.'

" She latterly subsisted on vegetables and small beverage."

John Ursulak, a silk-weaver, of Limburg, Prussia, died in 1812, aged 116.

" He was of *temperate* and sober habits."

John Wilson, of Worlingworth, Sussex, died in 1782, aged 116.

" For the last forty years of his life his suppers were almost uniformely made out of roasted *turnips;* to which vegetables, thus prepared, he always ascribed peculiar sanitary virtues."

Bernard le Borier de Fontanelle, of Rouen, France,

died in 1757, aged 100. He was a man of great talent, was Dean of the French Academy, Fellow of the Royal Society of London and of the Royal Academy of Berlin.

" Till upwards of ninety he does not appear to have experienced any of the maladies usually attendant upon old age. After this time he was subject to a periodical attack of fever in the spring, when he used to say, ' If I can only hold out till *strawberries* come in I shall get well.' He always *attributed his longevity* to a good *course of strawberry eating* every season."

Petratsch Zartan died in 1724, aged 185 years. He was born in 1537, at Kofroek, a village three miles from Temeswaer, in Hungary, where he lived 180 years.

" Being a member of the Greek Church, the old man was a strict observer of the numerous *fasts* established by its ritual, and was at all times *very abstemious in his diet,* save that once a day, with the milk and leaven cakes which constituted his sole food, he took a good-sized glass of brandy."

Galen, a physician of Pergamus, died about A.D. 270, aged 140.

He himself informs us that he always *ate* and drank *sparingly,* irrespective of his appetite, and although of delicate constitution, he attributed his longevity to his temperance.

Henry Hastings, Esq., second son of the Earl of Huntingdon, died in 1650, aged 100.

He was an original character, a great sportsman, and " never failed to eat *oysters* both at dinner and supper."

Marie Mallet, of Thènezay, France, died in 1845, aged 115.

" She was always very *abstemious* in her habits."

William Mead, M.D. (possibly grandfather of the celebrated Dr. Mead), died at Ware, Herts, in 1652, aged 148.

" He was distinguished for his great *temperance* and regular habits of life."

Mary Meigan, of Donaghmore, Ireland, died in 1813, aged 129.

" During the last thirty years of her life she lived apparently in the greatest penury and distress, *scarcely affording herself the means necessary for the keeping together of soul and body."* She, however, saved £1600.

Mr. R. Bowman, of Irthrington, near Carlisle, died in 1823, aged 118.

Bailey says : " He never used tea or coffee; his principal diet was bread, potatoes, hasty pudding, broth, and occasionally a little flesh meat. He scarcely ever tasted ale or spirits; his principal beverage was water, or milk and water mixed. It is right, however, to state that this *extreme abstemiousness* in all probability, arose as much from the desire to accumulate money as from the love of temperance."

Mrs. Barnett, widow, of Edgeworth Town, Ireland, died in 1809, aged 116.

" In her habits of *diet* she was always *very temperate."*

Bridget Devine, of Alean Street, Manchester, died in 1845, aged 147.

Her husband was a handloom weaver, and died

about twenty years before her. They were *very poor*, and after her husband's decease she was *supported* chiefly from the *parochial funds*.

Ephraim Pratt was living at Shaftesbury, U.S., in 1803, aged 116.

The Rev. T. Dwight states that this man was born at Sudbury, Mass., in 1687, and that throughout his life he had been *very temperate*, both in *diet* and habits. His general drink was *cider;* he was accustomed to take animal food, but in *less quantity* than most persons around him. Milk was also a common article of his diet.

The Hon. Mrs. Watkins, of Glamorganshire, died in 1790, aged 110.

" She was remarkable for regularity and *moderation*. For the last thirty years she subsisted entirely on potatoes."

Jonathan Hartop, of the village of Aldborough, near Boroughbridge, Yorkshire, died in 1790, aged 138.

" *He ate but little*, and his only beverage was milk."

Rebecca Joseph, of Malpas, near Newport, Monmouth, died the same year, aged 100.

" She lived a very *temperate life*. Her chief sustenance for the last two years was brown sugar and cold water."

Palcal Seria, died at Valentia, in 1791, aged 111.

" He subsisted towards the latter part of his life principally on *vegetables*, and frequently smoked tobacco."

Anne Froste, of West Raisin, Lincolnshire, died in 1722, aged 111.

"Married her last husband in her ninety-third year.
. . . For many years past she had lived on *milk and
tea diet.*"

Mr. Sherwood, of Stokesley, in Cleveland, died
in 1794, aged 105.

"By using much exercise, and by *temperate living,*
he enjoyed an unusual share of good health."

Mrs. Thomson, lived near Dublin, died in 1796,
aged 135.

"She was very active; and by a *regular mode of
living,* together with much exercise, attained so great
age."

A labourer, named Stender, died in 1792, in the
Duchy of Holstein, aged 103.

"His food, for the most part, was nothing but oatmeal and *buttermilk.*"

Baron Baravicio de Capellis, died in 1770, at Meran,
in Tyrol, aged 104.

"His usual food was *eggs;* he never tasted boiled
flesh; sometimes he ate a little roasted, but always in
very small quantity; and he drank abundance of tea
with rosa-solis, and sugar-candy."

Charles Macklin, of James Street, Covent Garden,
an eminent dramatic writer, and comedian of Covent
Garden Theatre, the veteran father of the stage, died
in 1797, aged 107. In the former part of his life he
lived intemperately; subsequent thereto, he determined to proceed by rule, which he scrupulously observed.

' *He was moderate at his meals,* and eat fish,
flesh, etc., till the age of seventy; when finding tea

did not agree with him, he substituted milk, with a little bread boiled in it, sweetened with brown sugar. . . . For the last forty years, his principal beverage was white wine and water, pretty sweet . . . He strictly observed the dictates of nature, ate when hungry, drank when thirsty, and slept when sleepy."
—*Vide* Memoirs of his life.

In the following cases, moderation and temperance may have been practised in diet, but not in alcoholic drinks and tobacco :

Daniel Bull McCarthy, lived in the county of Kerry, Ireland, died in 1752, aged 111.

" For the last seventy years, when in company, he drank *plentifully* of *rum* and *brandy*, which he called *naked truth*, and if, in compliance with solicitations, he drank claret or punch, he always drank an equal glass of rum or brandy, which he called a *wedge*."

Thomas Whittington, of Hellingdon, Middlesex, died in 1804, aged 104.

" Actually never took any other liquids, as liquids, into his stomach than ardent spirit—London gin; of which compound, until within a fortnight of his death, he took from a pint to a pint and a half daily."

Geo. Kirton, Esq., of Oxnop Hall, Yorkshire, died in 1764, aged 125.

He was a great foxhunter, and " no man, till within ten years of his death, made more free with the bottle."

Philip Laroque, of Frie, in Gascony, butcher, died in 1766, aged 102.

8

"Was drunk regularly twice a week till he was 100 years old."

William Thompson, of North Keyme, Lincolnshire, lived to 108.

" He smoked two pipes, and drank some ale, on the day of his death."

William Riddell, of Selkirk, in Scotland, died in 1718, aged 116.

This man was "remarkable for his love of brandy, which he drank in very large quantities. . . . He was not a drunkard (habitual), but he had frequent paroxysms of drinking, which continued several successive days. For the last two years of his life, his chief subsistence was a little bread infused in spirits and ale."

Pascal Seria, of Valentia, died at 111.

" Frequently smoked tobacco."

Richard Brown, of Peterchurch, Hereford, died in 1794, aged 108.

" In the instance of this old man, the assertion that smoking tobacco is prejudicial to health is completely refuted, as he was seldom seen without a pipe in his mouth, and took his last whiff a few hours before his death."

John Saunders, of Stratford, died in 1798, aged 106.

" He would walk to the Old Castle House, to drink a cup of ale and smoke his pipe."

John de la Somet, of Virginia, died in 1767, aged 130.

" He was a great smoker of tobacco, which, agreeing with his constitution, may not improbably be reckoned the cause of his uninterrupted health and longevity."

Joseph Creole, died in Caledonia, a little town of Wisconsin, on Jan. 27, 1866, aged 142.

" He was an inveterate smoker."

We do not advise either drinking or smoking, as a means of prolonging life; but still there is a philosophy noticed in the cases before us. Both drinking and smoking take away the appetite; less food is eaten, therefore a less amount of earthy salts are taken into the system, and the cause of old age is delayed in its results; still sufficient food is taken to support life, and great age follows.

Total abstainers must not forget that alcohol is formed in their own bodies, and, as Dr. Richardson says, " No man can be, in the strict scientific sense, a non-alcoholic, inasmuch as, ' will he, nill he,' he brews in his own economy a 'wee drap.' It is an innocent brew, certainly; but it is brewed, and the most ardent abstainer must excuse it. The fault, if it be one, rests with nature, who, according to our poor estimates, is no more faultless than the rest of her sex."

Alcohol in excess is injurious to health, especially to the mental capabilities—the reasons of which will be entered upon hereafter. But there is no evidence to show that alcohol in moderation, and judiciously used, is detrimental to health.

Tobacco affects the brain, the heart, circulation, and temperature. In excess it is therefore injurious. Tobacco is, to a certain extent, a disinfectant: it mitigates the pangs of hunger, and soothes depression. How often it calms the temper ! How many cross words are prevented in domestic life by the *moderate* use of tobacco !

Amongst other instances of longevity we have the Ancient Britons, whom Plutarch states "only *began to grow old* at 120 years."

"They were remarkable for their fine athletic form, for the great strength of their body, and for being swift of foot. They excelled in running, wrestling, climbing, and all kinds of bodily exercise; they were patient of pain, toil, and suffering of various kinds; were accustomed to fatigue, to bear hunger, cold, and all manner of hardships. They could run into morasses up to their necks, and live there for days without eating."—HENRY.

Boadicea, Queen of the Ancient Britons, in a speech to her army, when about to engage the degenerate Romans, said : "The great advantage we have over them is, that they cannot, like us, bear hunger, thirst, heat or cold ; they must have fine bread, wine, and warm houses ; to us every herb and root are food, every juice is our oil, and every stream of water our wine."

"Their arms, legs, and thighs were always left naked, and for the most part were painted blue. Their *food consisted almost exclusively of acorns, berries, and water*."—GOLDSMITH.

From the above, we may justly infer that the Ancient Britons lived on a diet which contained comparatively a small amount of earthy salts; further, the acorn contains tanno-gallate of potash, which would harden the albuminous and gelatinous structures : they would therefore be less liable to waste and decay. Their endurance of hunger, cold, and hardships, and their love of water (probably from a hardened state of the skin), cannot be considered as mere fables.

Louisa Truxo, a negress, was stated to be living in June, 1780, at Cordova, in the Tucuman, South America, aged 175.

The council of the city took every means to verify the authenticity of this statement:

"On examination of the woman, it appeared that she perfectly remembered having seen the prelate Fernando Truxo, her first master, who died in the year 1614; and that a year before his death he gave *her*, together with other property, towards a fund for founding the university of that place. As no registers of baptism existed so long back, care was taken to collect every circumstance that could be brought forward in corroboration of the woman's statements. One of these proofs was the deposition of another female negro, named Manuela, who was known to be 120 years old, and she declared that, when she was quite a child, she remembered that Louisa Truxo was then an elderly woman."

Thomas Carn, according to the parish register of the church of St. Leonard, Shoreditch, died January 28, 1588, aged 207 years.

He is stated "to have been born in the reign of Richard II., A.D. 1381, and lived in the reigns of twelve kings and queens of England."

The *Petersburg Gazette* published, in 1812, an instance of a man, in the diocese of Ekaterinoslau, having attained an age of more than 200 years.

Spotswood, Archbishop of St. Andrews, says that Saint Mungo always slept on the bare ground, and attained the extraordinary age of 185 years.

Mr. Evans, of Spital Street, Spitalfields, died in 1780, aged 139, in complete possession of all his faculties. He well remembered the execution of Charles I., being seven years old at the time. Bailey, writing in 1855, says : " What a wonderful link does such a life form between the present and the past ! There are, no doubt, numbers of persons still alive, at this time, who can well remember this remarkable old man. So that even the young men of this generation may be acquainted with individuals who knew the man who possibly witnessed an event which, at the present day, appears one of remote history."

" In the year 1566, a native of Bengal, named Numa de Cugna, died at the age of 370 years. He was a person of great simplicity, and quite illiterate, but of so extensive a memory that he was a kind of living chronicle, relating distinctly what had happened with his knowledge in the compass of his very long life, together with all the circumstances attending it."— MAFFEUS' " History of the Indies ;" and confirmed by Ferdinand Costequedo, Historiographer Royal of Portugal.

Thomas Parr, a native of Shropshire, died in 1635, aged 152. He married at the age of eighty-eight, " seeming no older than many at forty."

He was brought to London by Thomas, then Earl of

Arundel, to see Charles I, "when he fed high, drank
plentifully of wines, by which his body was *overcharged*,
his lungs obstructed, and the habit of the whole body
quite disordered; in consequence, there could not but
be speedy dissolution. If he had not changed his
diet, he might have lived many years longer."—
EASTON.

On his body being opened by Dr. Harvey, it was
found to be in a most perfect state. The heart was
thick, fibrous, and fat; his cartilages were not even
ossified, as is the case in all old people," and the only
cause to which death could be attributed was a " mere
plethora, brought on by more luxurious living in
London than he had been accustomed to in his native
country, where his food was plain and homely."

In a poem by John Taylor, on "the old, old, very
old man," the following outline of his diet is given :

> "He was of old Pythagoras' opinion,
> That green cheese was most wholesome with an *onion*,
> Coarse meslin bread, and for his daily swig,
> Milk, *buttermilk*, and water, *whey*, and whig.
> Sometimes metheglin, and for fortune happy,
> He sometimes supped a cup of ale most nappy."

He was married a second time at the age of a hundred
and twenty-one, and could run in foot-races and perform the ordinary work of an agricultural labourer
when 145 years old.

Henry Jenkins, of Ellerton, in Yorkshire, died in
1670, aged 169.

He remembered the battle of Flodden Field, in 1513,
at which time he was twelve years of age. The registers of the Chancery and other courts prove that he

gave evidence, and had an oath administered to him, 140 years before his death.

In the "Philosophical Transactions" of 1696, Sir Tancred Robinson states : "This Henry Jenkins, in the last century of his life, was a fisherman."

When ninety years of age, a child was born to him, and, when 160, he walked to London to have an audience with Charles II., and was able to swim across rapid rivers after he was 100. "His diet was coarse and *sour*."

Mrs. Clayton, of Springhead, died in 1867, aged 107 years.

"She was born in January, 1760. . . . Her health was uniformly good; she generally rose at six in the morning, and retired at nine in the evening, and walked often to Gravesend, a distance of three miles, without apparent fatigue."

Miguel Solis, of Bogota, San Salvador, now living, and whose age is supposed to be at least 180. At a congress of physicians, held at Bogota, Dr. Louis Hernandez read a report of his visit to this locally famous man, a country publican and farmer.

"We are told that he only confesses to this age (180 years); but his neighbours, who must be better able to judge, affirm that he is considerably older than he says. He is a half-bred, named Miguel Solis, and his existence is testified to by Dr. Hernandez, who was assured that when one of the 'oldest inhabitants' was a child, this man was recognised as a centenarian. His signature, in 1712, is said to have been discovered among those of persons who assisted in the construction of a certain convent (Franciscan convent, at San Sebastian). Dr. Hernandez found this wonderful individual working in his garden. His skin was like parchment, his hair as white as snow, and covering his head like a turban. He attributed his long life to his careful habits ; *eating only once a day*, for half an hour, because he believed that more food than could be eaten in half an hour could not be digested in twenty-four hours. He had been accustomed to *fast* on the first and fifteenth of every month, drinking, on those days, as *much water* as possible. He chose the most nourishing foods, and took all things cold."—*Lancet*, Sept. 7th, 1878.

From this and other sources we gather the following habits of this man :

1. He eats but once a day, and only for half an hour.

2. He eats meat but twice a month ; from which we may justly infer that he is to a certain extent abstemious in his daily meal.

3. He drinks large quantities of water.

4. He fasts two whole days every month.

From these habits it follows that, compared with the majority of mankind, he eats little, yet enough to support life; he therefore takes into his system a small amount of earthy compounds, which therefore take a longer period to accumulate, and produce the symptoms of decrepitude and old age at a far later period than they occur in most individuals who live upon an ordinary quantity of food, whose bodies become rigid, decrepit, and ossified, we will say, at about "threescore years and ten." Further, that his drinking large quantities of water, which, if not unusually hard, will tend to dissolve and remove those earthy compounds, which are not the *effect* but the *cause* of old age. We have not thought it necessary to make further inquiries concerning the diet and habits of this man. Our information is derived from numerous periodicals, and we only arrive at the above conclusions because we are convinced, from ascertained facts and experiments, that man may by diet alone attain the age which Miguel Solis is supposed to be.

Besides longevity, we notice in nature a power of restoration, which will be seen from the following cases :

Philip Laroque, to whom we have before referred—
" At the age of ninety-two, cut *four large teeth.*"

A Mr. Mazarella, of Vienna, died in 1774, aged 105.
" A few months before his death he had *several new teeth ;* and his *hair,* grown grey by age, *became black,* its original colour."

Numa de Cugna, the Bengalese tercentenarian before referred to—
" Had *four new sets of teeth ;* and the colour of his hair and beard had been frequently changed black to grey, and from grey to black."

Lord Bacon says the Countess of Desmond, who lived to 148, *renewed her teeth* once or twice.

Mary How, of Mapleton, Derby, died in 1751, from the effects of a fall from an apple-tree, aged 112.
" Two years before her death she *cut several new teeth,* and her *hair changed its colour.*"

Lady Angélique Domenqieux de Sempe, of Noniliac, in France, died in 1759, aged 103.

She "had *several new teeth* when near ninety years of age."

Susan Edmonds, of Winterbourne, Hants, died in 1780, aged 104.

"Five years before her death she had *new hair*, of a fine brown colour, which began to turn grey a few months before her death."

Sarah Williams, of Brent Torr, near Tavistock, died in 1809, aged 108.

"When in about her hundredth year, she cut *five new teeth*."

Elizabeth Spencer, widow, died in 1806, aged 105.

"For many years she was entirely deprived of sight; but about her one hundredth year she *recovered the use of her eyes*, which continued with her till the close of her life."

Janet Allan, of Kilmarnock, Ayrshire, died in 1788, aged 105 years.

"Four years before her death, her *sight*, which for long had been dim, in a great measure *returned*, so that she could see much better than had been the case for a number of years."

Owen Duffy, of Monaghan county, Ireland.

The *Dublin Freeman* of July 29, 1854, stated that this individual was then alive, aged 122 years. Having lost his second wife when he was 116, he married a third, a young woman, by whom he had a *son* and a *daughter*. At this time his youngest son was two years old, whilst his eldest was ninety.

Mrs. Jane Lewson, widow, of No. 12, Coldbath Square, London, died in 1816, aged 116.

She was left in affluent circumstances. Her apartments were never washed, her windows never cleaned, and she never practised ablutions of any kind whatever, for fear of taking cold. She "cut *two new teeth* at the age of eighty-seven."

Margaret Melvil, of Kettle, Fifeshire, died in 1783, aged 117.

"She *renewed several teeth* at a hundred years of age."

Marion Gibson, of Galston, died at 100.

"When she was about ninety years of age, she had a *new set of teeth.*"

Rebecca Poney, of the Poor-house, Norton Folgate, lived to 106.

"She cut *two new teeth* at the age of 102."

John Weeks, of New London, Connecticut, died at 114.

When he was 106, he married a girl of sixteen, at which time "his grey hairs had fallen off, which were renewed by a *dark* head of *hair ;* and several *new teeth* made their appearance."

John Rousey, Esq., of the island of Distrey, in Scotland, died in 1738, aged 137.

"He had a *son* at *one hundred* years of age, who inherited his estate."

John Riva, of Venice, died at 116.

"He always chewed citron-bark, and had a child after he was 100."

Margaret Krasiona, of the village of Koninia, in

Poland. When ninety-four years of age, she married her third husband, who was then 105.

"They lived together fourteen years, and had two boys and one girl. This is certified in the parish registers of the village of Ciwousin, district of Stensick, in the palatine of Sendomir."

Thomas Parr, when 102 years old, had a child by Catharine Milton, for which he did penance.

Dr. Stare states that his grandfather, a native of Bedfordshire, and who died in his hundredth year, "at the age of eighty-five had a *complete set of new teeth;* and his *hair,* from being of a snowy white, gradually *became darker.*"—"Philosophical Transactions," vol. xxiii.

"A magistrate named Bauborg, who lived at Rechingen, in the Palatinate, and who died in 1791, in the hundred and twentieth year of his age. In 1787, long after he had lost all his *teeth,* eight *new* ones *grew up*. At the end of six months they again dropped out, but their place was supplied by other new ones, both in the upper and the lower jaw; and nature, unwearied, continued this labour four years, and even till within a month of his death. After he had employed his new teeth for some time with great convenience in chewing his food, they took their leave, and new ones immediately sprung up in some of their sockets. All these teeth he acquired and lost without any pain; and the whole number of them amounted at least to fifty."—HUFELAND.

"The *Auxilia Breton* mentions a curious circumstance. It states that a gendarme named Labe, of the

Department of the Ilcuet Valaire, who had a grey
beard and hair, presented himself a few days ago perfectly black ! He said he had had a *determination of
blood to the head,* which caused his head to swell and
become black, as did also his beard and hair and part
of his body. He had felt great pain for a time, but
that afterwards he found himself much better; that
then his skin resumed its natural colour, but that the
hair and beard *remained black.* Two comrades of the
gendarme, one of them a corporal, confirmed his statements."—*Morning Advertiser.*

A patient of the author's, sixty-one years of age,
living in First Street, Chelsea, cut three new teeth in
the present year.

" By an inscription on a tombstone at Breslau, it
appears that one John Montanus, who was a dean there,
recovered three times the colour of his hair . . . Does it
therefore appear incredible or impossible that man may
occasionally after his 'three score years and ten,' again
exhibit the powers and physical qualities of youth ?"

A few years ago the *Times* gave an account of a
lady more than eighty years of age, who cut her *third
set of teeth,* and whose features were said to have the
juvenescence of thirty years.

The above-mentioned cases are but a few of many
which have been collected. We cannot therefore consider
such changes impossible; nature has repeatedly accomplished them, apparently by accident; but what nature
accomplishes apparently by accident, may become a
possibility, if we are able to discover the laws and principles which govern such changes, and if we are
further able to apply them and regulate their action.

In the animal kingdom we find numerous cases of longevity : the first we notice is in reptiles, which are cold-blooded, with slight powers of respiration, and whose internal and external consumption is therefore much less than in warm-blooded animals. They are very tenacious of life, and most of them have a power of reproducing and restoring destroyed organs ; thus earthworms restore themselves after being cut with a spade ; the head and horns of a snail will grow again in six months ; the limbs and tail of a water-newt are replaced in a few months, and even if its eye is destroyed, another is perfected in about ten months.

" A toad was found at Organ, in France, in a well which had been covered up for 150 years. It was torpid, but revived on being exposed. Many well-authenticated cases are recorded of toads found alive in old stones and in old trees, where they must have lived for many centuries."—SIR RICHARD PHILLIPS.

The "Transactions of the Swedish Academy" give an account of a toad found in 1733 in a stone quarry, seven ells deep in the middle of a hard block of stone, and which was extricated with much labour by hammer and chisel, and was alive, though very weak. Its skin is described as being shrivelled, "covered here and there with a stony crust."

" The *testudo* or tortoise is so long-lived that two are recorded in England who lived 120 and 200 years . . . In the library of Lambeth Palace is the shell of a tortoise, brought there in 1623. It lived till 1730, and was then accidentally killed. Another in the palace at Fulham, procured by Bishop Laud in 1628, died in

1753. One at Peterborough lived 220 years."—Sir R. Phillips.

The crocodile and alligator, which many travellers assert increase in size as long as they exist, from what is at present known, seem to live to very great ages.

Serpents live to almost incredible ages, and many believe they never die from "natural causes."

"When it (the serpent) is old, by squeezing itself between two rocks, it can strip off its old skin, and so grows *young again*."—Calmet's "Dictionary."

"Snakes, frogs, lizards, etc., cast their skin every year; and it appears that this method of becoming again young contributes very much to their support and duration."—Hufeland.

Many reptiles cast their skins; this is especially noticed in snakes. In casting its skin a large quantity of gelatinous and earthy matter, which by their accumulation have gradually given rise to the characteristics of "old age," is thrown off; the animal is relieved of them, and becomes in the full sense of the term young again.

Crabs and lobsters undergo a rejuvenescence in casting their shells annually; and for about four days they are naked and defenceless. Their size increases only when in this soft state; their mail, which contains a large quantity of earthy matter, soon prevents further expansion until it is cast off, when the animal is again allowed to increase in size.

In fishes many instances of extraordinary longevity are recorded, which is especially marked in those of slow growth.

"Carp grow but two or three inches *per annum*, and

live to a great age; some in the lake at Fontainebleau being two or three hundred years old. . . . Whales live many centuries."—"Million of Facts."

"We know from the ancient Roman history, that in the imperial fish-ponds there were several lampreys (muraenae) which had attained to their sixtieth year; and which had at length become so well acquainted and familiar with man, that *Crassus, orator, unam ex illis defleverit.*"*—HUFELAND.

"The pike, a dry, exceedingly voracious animal, and carp also, according to undeniable testimony, prolong their life to 150 years. The salmon grows rapidly and dies soon. On the other hand, the perch, the growth of which is slower, preserves its existence longer."—*Ibid.*

"Gesner says that the longevity of the pike is almost incredible; he mentions as an instance one that was taken in Hailborn, in Swabia, in the year 1497, with these words engraven on a ring: 'I am the fish that was first of all put into this lake by Frederick Second, Oct. 5th, 1230.' This gave it the age of two hundred and sixty-seven years."—RHIND'S "Six Days of Creation."

"Some species of fish and certain snakes are said to live till some accident puts an end to their *indefinite term of life.*"—SOUTHEY.

In birds a renovation is noticed in the process of moulting, during which the old feathers are cast off, and with them fibrinous, gelatinous and earthy substances, and new feathers are acquired, which, by their

---

* That Crassus, the orator, shed tears for one of them when it died.

growth remove certain quantities of these solid substances from the system.

Many cases of longevity are recorded in birds, especially those which live on fruits, fish and other animal foods.

It is affirmed that some of the parrot species live in their natural state to "ages ranging from five to seven hundred years."

"One has instances of its living sixty years a prisoner with man, and how old may it not have been when it was caught ?"

"The swan lives 200 years ;" some authorities even prolong this to 300.

"Some time ago, a male swan, which had seen many generations come and go, and witnessed the other mutations incidental to the lapse of 200 years, died at Rosemount. He was brought to Dunn when the late John Erskine, Esq., was in his infancy, and was then said to be 100 years old. About two years ago he was purchased by the late David Duncan, Esq., of Rosemount, and within that period his mate brought him forth four young ones, which he destroyed as soon as they took the water. Mr. Mallison Bridget (in whose museum the bird is now to be seen) thinks it might have lived much longer but for a lump or excrescence at the top of the windpipe, which, on dissecting him, he found to be composed of grass and tow. This is the same bird that was known and recognised in the early years of octogenarians in this and the neighbouring parishes by the name of the ' Old Swan of Dunn.' "— *Medical Gazette.*

In 1782 " Farmer Pope, of Beaminster, Dorset, had

a goose eighty-six years old, which had been on the farm with four successive tenants.''

The raven, rook, crow, hawk, seagull, pelican, heron, crane, and other birds of a similar nature, are believed to live beyond a hundred years.

Tacitus says the eagle lives to 500 years, and there are instances of its having lived in confinement more than 100, and one died at Vienna aged 104.

" A gentleman at London a few years ago received from the Cape of Good Hope one (a falcon) that had been caught with a golden collar, on which was inscribed in English, ' His Majesty K. James of England. An. 1610.'' It had therefore been at liberty 182 years from the time of its escape. How old was it when it escaped ? It was of the largest species of these birds, and possessed still no little strength and spirit ; but it was remarked that its eyes were blind and dim, and that the feathers of its neck had become white.''— HUFELAND.

In the *mammalia* the elephant perhaps attains the greatest age.

" They grow for thirty or forty years, and live 200 or 300 ; some say 400 years.''

An elephant called Hannibal died in 1859, in a travelling circus in America. " He was extremely old. We have heard his age stated variously at from 500 to 1000 years.''*

After Alexander the Great had vanquished Porus, King of India, he took a large elephant which had fought valiantly in battle for the king, and called him Ajax,

---

* Reynolds' "Miscellany."

dedicating him to the sun, and setting him free with the following inscription :

" Alexander, the son of Jupiter, hath dedicated Ajax to the sun."

This elephant was found 350 years afterwards with the inscription.

Speaking of the longevity of the elephant, Thomson says :

> " With gentle might endued,
> Though powerful, yet not destructive ; here he sees
> Revolving ages sweep the changeful earth,
> And empires rise and fall ; regardless he
> Of what the never-resting race of man project."

Elephants " live on vegetables," and in their natural state are very fond of the young and tender shoots and leaves of trees; their diet is therefore one adapted to longevity.   Moreover, the tusk or tooth " weighs from 120 to 200 lbs.," and one hundred parts contain twenty-four of gelatine and sixty-four of carbonate of lime; the tusks therefore relieve the system of an elephant of from nearly 80 to 128 lbs. of lime ; these are further-more *cast*, being found in the woods of Africa and Ceylon, but how often and at how long a period is as yet undetermined.

The wild hog lives chiefly on roots, and is said to live in its native state " to the age of 300 years."

A " lion lived seventy years in the Tower ;" we may therefore justly infer, that in its natural state it lives beyond a century.

The camel " generally attains the age of fifty, and sometimes of 100 years."   " It eats *little* and drinks less."

"They require *little* and coarse food, and live for ten or fifteen days without water."

The horse in his wild state lives to upwards of fifty years; but when brought to subjugation by the severity of man, he seldom attains half this age.

It is a well-known fact that when a horse does little work, and passes the greater part of his days—especially the early ones—in his pasture, he lives to nearly forty years; but when a horse is hard worked and the process of transpiration thereby increased, and is moreover fed upon beans, oats, and other "ossifying" foods, his days are much shorter; few in fact reach twenty years, and even "Eclipse," a race-horse which for speed is said to have never been defeated, with all the attention man could bestow, died at twenty-five years.

This faithful servant of man soon becomes prematurely old from the diet on which he is fed, in fact his food contains so much earthy matter that concretions (hippolithi) of phosphates of lime, magnesia, and ammonium, in the cæcum are of very common occurrence; the deposition of earthy salts in the system is also accelerated by hard work, which increases the process of transpiration.

From the above few cases of the ages of reptiles, birds, and animals, which we have selected as illustrations, it is clear that those of them which attain the greatest longevity in animated nature are those which are subject to or possessed of one or more of the following peculiarities or qualities :

1. Those which are only slightly susceptible to the action of atmospheric *oxygen*.

2. Those which are possessed of a *restorative* power, or are enabled to throw off from the system fibrinous, gelatinous, and earthy matter, and the more perfect this renovation, the greater the duration of life.

3. Those which subsist upon food which contains a small quanity of earthy compounds.

4. Those which eat but little or seldom.

In the vegetable kingdom are numerous instances of longevity.

" A lime in the Grisons is fifty-one feet round and about 600 years old."

" A dragon's-blood tree in Teneriffe was forty-eight feet round and 1000 years old."

" The *cubbeer burr*, near Baroach, has 350 main trunks and 3000 small ones. It is believed to be 3000 years old."

One specimen of the African *baobab* was estimated by its circles to be 5700 years old by Adanson and Humboldt.

Adanson found some of these trees only six feet in diameter with the names of seafaring men who visited them in the fifteenth and sixteenth centuries, cut on them, and with the incisions little extended.

There is a cypress in Mexico 120 feet round, which De Canolle considers older than Adanson's baobab.

The yew attains great age, those "at Fountain's Abbey are about 1200 years old ;" one "at Crowhurst 1500 ;" one at Fortingal above 2000 years ; and one at Braburn the age of which is stated to be from 2500 to 3000 years.

" A chestnut in Gloucestershire is 900, and one at Saucerre 600 years."

" Terebinth-trees, the El-Elah of the Bible, live 1500 or 2000 years, but neglect has rendered them scarce in Syria."

A chestnut was planted in 800 at Tamworth; it was a boundary called the "Great Chestnut-tree" in the reign of Stephen, in 1135, and "in 1759 it bore nuts, which produced young trees;" it was stated to be fifty-two feet round.

" Two orange-trees at Rome, planted by St. Dominick and Thomas Aquinas, are from 500 to 600 years old."

An apple-tree was stated to be in existence in 1820 at Woolstrope, "from which Newton saw an apple fall in 1665."

Ivys have been recorded which have lived five hundred years, and the elm, larch, and other trees are stated to live the same or even a longer period.

The oak is slow of growth and reaches a great age. De Canolle states that there are oaks in France 1500 years old. The Wallace oak, near Paisley, is more than 700 years old.

" Some olives, near Jerusalem, are 800 years old."

Throughout the animal and vegetable kingdoms, with a few exceptions, which would be too lengthy to enter upon in the present work, a similar cause of natural death is observed to that which we have traced to man; and even the stately and venerable oak, which inspires us with reverence and awe when we contemplate that the tree we gaze upon perhaps once shaded our wild ancestors and the Druids, only dies because the central and oldest parts of the wood gradually acquire such compactness, hardness, and want of porosity, that it becomes incapable of imbibing or receiving further nourishment; a process analogous to "induration" and "ossification" in man and animals.

CHAPTER V.

AGENTS BEST ADAPTED FOR A LENGTHENED PROLONGATION OF EXISTENCE.

By the term *agents* best adapted to prolong life we mean those substances or compounds which, by their action in or upon the system, tend to check the *cause* of "old age," and "natural death," and which tend to prevent or even remove the accumulations which we have already shown are not the *effect*, but the *cause* of the changes which are observed as age advances, either by preventing the excessive action of atmospheric *oxygen*, or by removing *earthy* compounds, which have accumulated to an extent more than is requisite to supply the wants of the system, or those substances which combine the two actions.

To commence with *solvents*, or those agents which tend to prevent the accumulation of earthy matter in the system, the first we notice is *water*.

When water is decomposed by electricity, the hydrogen at the negative pole is double the volume of the oxygen at the positive pole; water, therefore, is composed in bulk of one volume of oxygen and two volumes of hydrogen; but oxygen being sixteen times as heavy as hydrogen, eight parts of oxygen by weight unite with one part of hydrogen to form water. We may justly term water an *oxide of hydrogen.*

Water exists in nature in three forms; in the solid as ice, in the liquid as water, and in the gaseous as steam. The greater part of the water existing in nature is undergoing a slow but constant process of distillation, condension, and redistillation; it rises from the evaporation of the waters of the earth in the form of steam, to become clouds; these again condense and fall as rain, sleet, snow, or hail.

Rain-water is the purest form of water occurring in nature; however, even during its fall to the surface of the earth it acquires impurities from the air, but directly it touches the land it falls upon it dissolves some of the materials with which it comes in contact, and becomes still more impure. Most salts are more or less soluble in water, which is the most general solvent of chemical substances in nature; rain-water thus dissolves and combines with portions of the soluble constituents from the strata through which it percolates, and becomes spring-water or river-water, and ultimately passes into the sea, to again take part in this vast process of distillation. The solid matter in solution in water is deposited when the water is evaporated; in order to obtain pure water it is therefore necessary to *distil* it, that is, to boil it, and collect the water produced by the condensation of the steam.

So great are the solvent properties of distilled water, that when water is distilled in glass or earthenware vessels, it dissolves small quantities of substance of the vessel in which it is condensed; and if retorts be so arranged that distillation and redistillation from one vessel to the other may be carried on, and further, if this process is often repeated, a sediment will be found at the bottom of each vessel. The sediment formed part of the vessels in which the process was carried on, was dissolved by the water on its condensation, and was deposited when it evaporated; and the oftener the distillation is repeated, the greater is the deposit.

This fact led many of the Grecian philosophers to refer all things to water, for they conceived that solid matter *originated* even from distilled water. In fact that all solid matter was at one time in aqueous solution.

The process of boiling spring-water, or river-water, precipitates part of the solid matters it contains, especially those salts which are held in solution by an excess of carbonic acid (if carbonates be present).

Most drinking waters contain *lime* to a greater or a less extent, in some form or other, generally as carbonate, or sulphate; and those waters which contain lime to any extent should be avoided for drinking purposes. The *alkaline* salts contained in many waters do not accumulate in the system; they are therefore not injurious, but many of them are beneficial.

There are many recorded cases of longevity which may be distinctly traced to drinking large quantities of water.

The Seres, expressly called *Macrobii*, or the ancient Chinese, lived to extraordinary ages, and Lucian ascribes their longevity to their " drinking water in great abundance."

The idea which was held centuries ago, that *dew* *
water collected from the mountains, and used as a
drink, would prolong life, is a very correct one; it is a
distilled water of nature, and whether it is charged
with electricity or not, is very invigorating.

Distilled water, used as a drink, is absorbed directly
into the blood, the solvent properties of which it increases to an extent that it will keep salts already
existing in the blood in solution, prevent their undue
deposition in the various organs and structures, and
favour their elimination by the different *excretæ*. If
the same be taken in large quantities, or if it be the
only liquid taken into the system, either as a drink or
as a medium for the ordinary decoctions of tea, coffee,
etc., it will in time tend to remove those earthy compounds which have accumulated in the system, the
effects of which usually become more manifest as the
age of forty or fifty years is attained.

The daily use of distilled water facilitates the removal of deleterious compounds from the body by
means of the excretæ, and therefore tends to the prolongation of existence.

The use of distilled water may be especially recommended after the age of thirty-five or forty years is
attained; it will of itself prevent many diseases to
which mankind is especially subject to after this age;
and were it generally used, gravel, stone in the bladder,
and other diseases due to the formation of calculi in
different parts of the system, would be much more
uncommon.

* Dew is the condensation of aqueous vapour by a body which
has *radiated* its atomic motion of heat below the temperature
of the surrounding atmosphere.

Vessels, or retorts, used for the distillation of water for drinking purposes, should be made of iron, not of glass or earthenware.

Lactic acid is produced by natural or artificial fermentation from milk, or other animal matter containing lactose, or milk-sugar. In a pure state it is a syrupy liquid, transparent, and inodorous, soluble in water, alcohol, and ether. When distilled, it decomposes, unless atmospheric air be excluded, when it may be distilled unchanged.

Milk holds in solution cheese or caseine, the solubility of which is dependent upon the presence of *alkaline phosphates,* and *free alkalies,* and not upon *earthy* salts. The neutralisation of the alkali by an acid causes the cheese to separate. Fermentation may be naturally or artificially communicated to the milk-sugar, which is present in the milk, the elements of which are transposed into lactic acid, which neutralises the alkali and causes the caseine to separate.

The caseine, or cheese-curd, contains nearly all the phosphate of lime and earthy matter, but only part of the *alkaline* phosphates of the milk; but the liquid, or *whey,* contains the remaining *alkaline phosphates, lactates,* and the *lactic acid.*

Buttermilk is milk deprived of its butter, or oily part, the milk-sugar of which has been more or less converted into lactic acid. It appears to be generally given to pigs, but formerly it was largely used as an article of human consumption, and it has many good points which recommend it as a food for invalids, and as a dietetic article for more general use.

Lactic acid forms a definite series of salts with the

alkaline and *earthy* bases, and has a great tendency to prevent the undue accumulation of earthy matter in the system. There are also many instances of extraordinary longevity, which may be traced solely to lactic acid contained in whey, or buttermilk, used as a continued article of diet, several instances of which we have given in the preceding chapter.

Amongst other solvents we have the mineral acids, sulphuric, nitric, hydrochloric, and phosphoric. With the exception of the latter (phosphoric acid), the mineral acids, in large buantities, are foreign to the system, and their continued use is injurious. The action of phosphoric acid will be entered into when we consider phosphorus.

Amongst those substances which prevent the excessive action of atmospheric oxygen, or the waste of the system, we first notice *tannin*, which has the power of tanning, hardening, and rendering the albuminous gelatinous structures of the body more leather-like in character, and less liable to decay.

Tannic and gallic acids alone are objectionable, and their continued use produces dyspepsia. Their combination with an alkali to a certain extent removes this objection, and they exist in nature, combined with *potash*, in the walnut, acorn, etc., the action of which we have already noticed when speaking of the longevity and diet of the ancient Britons.

Potash alum, a combination of sulphate of alumina and sulphate of potash, has a similar astringent action if taken in small doses. This remark does not apply to the *ammonia* alum which is generally used in the present day on account of its cheapness; sulphate of ammonia, which is largely produced in our gas-works, is here substituted for the sulphate of potash of the potash alum.

Fresh brewers' yeast has a great affinity for oxygen, and would undoubtedly prevent undue oxidation or waste of the tissues. Within the last few years it has been employed medicinally, with good effect, in many diseases which are characterised by excessive oxidation.

The alkalies, *potash* and *soda*, have the property of increasing the solubility of albumen and fibrin. The continued use of soda is depressing. The best preparation of the alkalies for this purpose is the liquor potassæ, in small doses of five or ten drops largely diluted with water. It acts also as an antacid and antilithic; but its continued use renders the fluids and urine so alkaline, that deposits of earthy phosphates may possibly result from this alkalinity; but this deposit, which is chiefly noticeable in the urine, is dependent solely upon diet—or the quantity of earthy phosphates taken into the system as food, and is to a great extent preventible by the conjoined use of the vegetable acids, and entirely by phosphoric acid, as a citrate, tartrate, or phosphate. Phosphoric acid undergoes no alteration in passing through the system, and is therefore traceable to the secretions and excretions. But vegetable acids are not found in either; they are, as it were, burnt up in the system, and resolved into carbonic acid and water. This action *lowers* the temperature of the body and increases the fluidity of the blood, and this is the reason that the vegetable acids act so beneficially in many forms of fever, and not because they neutralise ammonia, which is found in excess in the blood in most fevers, and which neutralisation, did it exist, could only last for a short period.

The vegetable acids, either alone or combined with alkalies as they exist in fruits, or artificially prepared, as before stated, tend to prolong life—firstly, by decreasing the temperature of the body, therefore the waste of the system; secondly, on the combustion of the acid, the alkali being left free, the solubility of albumen and fibrin existing in both the blood and the tissues is increased, there is a lessened tendency to their deposit—to the formation of fibrinous and gelatinous accumulations in the system.

Amongst the agents which combine the *two* actions, the only one we can recommend is *phosphorus*, because it is a substance not foreign to the system. When phosphorus is in a *free* state, owing to its great affinity for oxygen it unites with it in the system, thereby decreasing the waste, decomposition, or oxidation of the body, and forms acids which prevent the accumulation of earthy compounds, and facilitate their elimination from the system.

Phosphorus, owing to its great affinity for oxygen, does not occur free in nature, except in the most highly organised structures of animals and a few plants; apart from these, it exists only in a state of combination always with oxygen, and with an alkaline or earthy base, generally as phosphate of lime, which is found largely in mountains in Spain and other parts of the world. Phosphate of lime is the principal constituent of apatite, phosphorite, coprolites, etc., and exists in most structures throughout the animal and vegetable kingdoms ; and, in conjunction with other earthy compounds, plays a great part in causing their death by its accumulation.

In the animal kingdom it is taken into the system in the articles of diet derived generally from vegetables ; and, in the vegetable kingdom, by imbibition or absorption from the earth.

Phosphorus was accidentally discovered by Brandt, of Hamburg, in 1669 ; but Scheele obtained it from bones, and examined its properties, in 1769. It is generally prepared from powdered bone-ash, or phosphate of lime, by adding to it about two-thirds of its weight of sulphuric acid and about sixteen parts of water. By this means the bone-ash is decomposed ; the sulphuric acid unites with part of the lime, forming sulphate of lime, which is insoluble and precipitates, whilst the greater part of the phosphorus is left in combination with oxygen, hydrogen, and the remaining lime forming superphosphate of lime which remains in solution. This solution is then evaporated to the consistence of a syrup, and mixed with charcoal ; it is then placed in earthenware retorts, the necks of which, to prevent the admission of atmospheric oxygen, are placed under water. It is then heated to redness, when carbonic acid gas is liberated, and about half the phosphorus distils over and falls as yellowish drops to the bottom of the water, whilst the other half remains in the retorts, in combination with the lime, as a pyrophosphate.

The phosphorus thus prepared is generally purified by redistillation, and by pressing it through leather under hot water ; but the phosphorus thus purified

generally contains so many impurities that it is unfit
for medicinal use. The chief impurity is arsenic, but
bismuth, copper, and cobalt are often found in what is
known as "commercial" phosphorus. For internal
use it therefore requires further purification. When
phosphorus has been passed through leather, boiling in *liquor potassœ* will readily remove the arsenic,
forming a *liquor arsenicalis*. It should then be mixed
with vegetable charcoal, redistilled, and allowed to fall
into lime-water. It should then be washed, or well
agitated, in *liquor ammoniœ fortis*. What slight impurities may now be present, will readily be removed
by adding a mixture composed of equal parts of charcoal and *carbonate of iron*, making this into a paste
and redistilling, when irregular masses of *pure* phosphorus are obtained.

Phosphorus readily oxidises, and slight friction, or
sometimes the heat of the hand, will cause its ignition.
It unites with oxygen in four proportions, forming
oxide of phosphorus, hypophosphorous acid, phos-
phorous acid, and phosphoric acid.

"When phosphorus is kept for a time near its
boiling-point, air being excluded, it undergoes a *true
coagulation*, and, at the same time, a change in its most
striking properties."—LIEBIG.

If common phosphorus be exposed to a temperature
between 464° and 482° F., for some hours, atmospheric
air being excluded, or in an atmosphere such as
hydrogen or carbonic acid, which will not act chemically on it, it becomes a solid dark red and opaque
substance, exactly *equal in weight* to the common

phosphorus used, but differing greatly from it in properties. This is what is called *amorphous phosphorus*.

The ordinary phosphorus is easily fusible, very inflammable in contact with air, is luminous in the dark, is readily oxidised, and slowly passes in the air into a deliquescent acid; whilst the altered, red, or amorphous phosphorus is not inflammable, and does not take fire until sufficient heat is used to reconvert it into the ordinary form; it is not luminous, and is not changed in moist air.

Bisulphuret of carbon dissolves common phosphorus in all proportions, but the altered phosphorus is insoluble in it.

Common phosphorus has distinct actions upon the animal system, and, in excess, is very poisonous; the same quantity of the altered phosphorus is inert, and has no action whatever on the body.

At a *low red heat*, the altered or amorphous phosphorus is *reconverted* into the ordinary form.

"Now, what is the *cause* of these transformations in the properties of this element? What is the mysterious part played here by heat? We can explain difference of properties in two compounds of the same composition, by a difference in the arrangement of their atoms; and this view in many cases is unquestionably correct. But how is it with phosphorus, which we must regard as an elementary body? *Is phosphorus, perhaps, really a compound?* These remarkable phenomena are as yet obviously unexplained; but they open up to us a world of new ideas."
—LIEBIG.

Phosphorus *in the air* gives off white fumes, which are luminous in the dark: these fumes are due to combustion or oxidation; but phosphorus is luminous *in vacuo*, and the more complete the vacuum, the greater is the luminosity.   Here oxygen plays no part—phosphorus is luminous *per se*; its luminosity, therefore, is not necessarily due to oxidation.

If albumen or white of egg be kept for a time at its boiling-point, it coagulates; *a something* (a vitality?) imperceptible, imponderable, and not necessarily chemical, has gone—it is eliminated by the heat, and the character and properties of the albumen are changed.   This *something*, or a something analogous, may be given back to it either by animal digestion, or artificially by chemical means, when its former properties are restored, and it becomes again true or fluid albumen coagulable by heat.

When phosphorus is kept for some hours at its boiling-point, "it undergoes a true coagulation;" a *something** imperceptible and imponderable has gone.

---

* A similar instance is seen in the diamond, although "when heated strongly in a medium incapable of acting chemically upon it, the diamond swells up, and is converted into a black mass resembling coke," and also, when burnt in oxygen, carbonic acid alone is formed—showing it to consist of pure carbon. The diamond is not pure carbon alone, for a *something* imponderable is driven off by heat, and pure carbon is left exactly the same in weight as the diamond; we have, therefore, discovered the means of eliminating this *something* from the diamond, but we have not as yet been able to replace it, or to unite carbon and this imponderable something.   When this is discovered, we shall be enabled to make diamonds artificially: and were a man to make this end his object, we see nothing to

10—2

The weight is exactly the same; but the continued heat has eliminated a *something*, and the properties of the phosphorus are changed. A higher temperature gives back this *something*, and the phosphorus again assumes its former characters. But as phosphorus on its combustion gives off electricity, we may justly infer that this *something* which is eliminated is *electricity*. Again, as phosphorus is luminous in a vacuum, totally independent of oxidation, it would be neither theoretical nor speculative to say that we need not regard phosphorus as an elementary body, but that it is really a compound, of which *light* in the abstract form and *electricity* are important constituents.

The light in this case is light *per se*—it does not originate in heat—the motion of the radiation of atoms; nor does it arise from combustion or any combination of gases. It is luminous when removed from all chemical action.

It has been shown in the present century that *light* is an originator of motion; this is instanced in the little instrument invented by Mr. Crooke, which rotates under the influence of the sun's rays, and the more intense the light, the greater the rapidity of the motion. This instrument is constructed for the purpose, and instances the action of light upon *dead* matter; what, therefore, may be the influence of light upon *living* matter !

---

prevent his success. Its discoverer would perhaps be struck with amazement, but he might also be amused at its simplicity.

Phosphorus exists in the most highly developed organs or structures of man and animals.

"The *brain* and other nerve-centres contain a substance termed *protagon*, of which *phosphorus* forms an essential constituent. It crystallises in microscopic needles, and is very easily decomposed. Amongst the *products* of decomposition of protagon are glycerine, *phosphoric acid*, and several fatty acids, and an ammonium base called *neurine*."—ROSCOE.

Now, certain proportions of phosphorus exist in the brain in a free or unoxidised form, and within the last few years we see it stated that the protagon of the brain and nervous system contains its phosphorus as a hypophosphite. This error may easily be accounted for from the fact that protagon readily decomposes, and the phosphorus combining with oxygen would be found as a hypophosphite, or even as a phosphate or as phosphoric acid, if the brain were not in a fresh state. However, difference of opinion is not needed on this point, as a very simple experiment will decide the question.

If we take a *fresh* brain (either human or animal), and immerse it in either absolute alcohol, sulphuric ether, or olive oil, we obtain a *luminous* solution of phosphorus; a phosphate is not luminous, a hypophosphite is not luminous, *free* phosphorus is luminous. The brain, therefore, contains free or unoxidised phosphorus.

We naturally inquire for what purpose phosphorus exists in this form, in the largest quantity, in structures of the highest organisation—as, for instance, the brain, which, as an established physiological fact, presides over every thought and action of our material bodies.

The first *cause* of thought is not organic, it has a higher origin, the nature of which we are as yet unacquainted with; and as Hufeland, a philosophic physician, said a century ago, "The first *cause* of *thought* is spiritual; but the *business of thinking* itself, as carried on in this mortal machine, is *organic*."

Now, the brain contains cells, some larger than others, and variously shaped. The brain also contains fibres, some of which are tubular, and have a covering membrane, and some of which have not, called respectively *tubular* and *gelatinous* fibres. Some of these fibres are joined to and issue from the cells; this is undoubtedly the case with some of the *caudate* or larger cells which have tail-like processes, some of which "become continuous, with an ordinary nerve fibre." This is not always the case, nor is it necessary to have direct continuity. Contact is all we require; and most, if not all, the fibres of the brain are in *contact* with cells. Here in the brain, spinal marrow, and nerves, we see a most perfect *telegraphic* apparatus—nature's design, and which is distributed by means of the nerves and their subdivisions—arborescent ramifications to every part of the body, and which we may compare to a set of *telegraph wires*.

During thought, mental exertion, worry, remorse, or hard study, *phosphates* are largely increased in the *excretæ;* and as the brain is the centre of these thoughts and ideas, we may justly infer that this increase of phosphates is due to oxidation or loss of phosphorus from the brain—that the *first* effect of thought is to cause oxidation of phosphorus during the "*business of thinking* itself."

Now, it is a chemico-physiological fact that the brain contains phosphorus.

It is a chemical fact that on the oxidation or burning up of phosphorus in the atmosphere an electric charge is given off.

It is a demonstrable fact that on passing a current of electricity along the course of one or more nerves of an animal body, spasmodic actions, muscular contractions, are the result.

It is, therefore, clear that phosphorus plays a more important action in the animal economy than has heretofore been supposed; and that thought, the mind itself, many nervous actions with which the mind has no connection, and volition and common sensation, are intimately connected with the presence of phosphorus in the cerebro-spinal axis.

As an instance of this, we may ask: What is *motion* caused by will? A man puts forth his hand to reach a certain object. Phosphorus is oxidised in the brain in cells, which either communicate, or are in contact with nerve fibres, and the electric* current

* In the study of an eminent philosopher, named De Luc, a suspended ball was kept in regular pulsation for years by means of successive accumulations of electricity from a dry pile, the discharges being carried off by the ball. Phosphorus must of necessity be gradually oxidised in the cerebro-spinal axis, even in sleep ; electricity must develop, and when it has reached a certain tension, must be discharged along the nerves which supply the heart, and thus cause its pulsation, and the resulting circulation of the blood. A similar conclusion was arrived at by Sir John Herschel, also by Dr. Arnott ; but neither of them showed a *source* of the required electrical power.

caused by the oxidation of phosphorus in the brain passes down these fibres (on exactly the same principle as the telegraph wire) to the arm or hand, contractions of muscles in the limb result—the action he willed is completed.

"Every thought, every sensation is accompanied by a change in the composition of the substance of the brain."—LIEBIG.

"According to careful estimates, three hours of hard study wear out the body more than a whole day of hard physical exertion. 'Without phosphorus, no thought,' is a German saying; and the consumption of that essential ingredient of the brain increases in proportion to the amount of labour which this organ is required to perform. The wear and tear of the brain are easily measured by careful examination of the salts of the liquid excretions."—*Boston Journal of Chemistry*.

The importance of the brain is again verified by the fact that although it only weighs, on an average, one-fortieth of the weight of the body, one-fifth of the blood goes to supply this organ. Now does the brain, as is generally believed, derive its supply of phosphorus from earthy or alkaline phosphates taken into the system in the articles of diet? Is there any action existing in the body which has the power to de-oxidise phosphates and extract free phosphorus?

"The mean temperature of man is 98° 6';" and the only means we have at present of artificially preparing phosphorus from phosphates is by detaching the oxygen by charcoal at a *red heat*, a temperature which could not exist in any living organism; nor is there any electric action in the body of sufficient force for this purpose.

" *Light* separates the moisture in plants into its constituent hydrogen and oxygen, and it disengages the oxygen from the carbonic acid, so as to deposit the carbon in union with hydrogen—as gum, resin, and oil, which forms their ligneous parts. Consolidation and vigour *depend on light.*"

" The retention of oxygen, for want of *light*, renders plants white. . . . Solar light is the agent by which the carbonic acid in gas is decomposed."

" The life of every created being is the more perfect the more it enjoys the influence of *light*. Let a plant or an animal be deprived of light, notwithstanding every nourishment, care, and cultivation, it will first lose its colour, then its strength, and at last entirely decay. Even man, who passes his life in darkness, becomes pale, relaxed, and heavy, and at length loses the whole *energy of life;* as is proved by the many melancholy instances of persons shut up in gloomy dungeons."

In darkness there is no expansion of organised life, except at the expense of putrefaction and decomposition, resulting only in the production of vegetation of the most imperfect kind ; apart from this, no form of life is generated of a higher order—nothing feels, nothing breathes.

" The phosphoric light seen in the ocean is caused by innumerable quantities of *phosphoric* insects (*noctiluca miliaris*), and is sometimes so intense as to make the waves appear like red-hot balls."

" Owen describes cylindrical flexible mollusca, in

the sea near Benguela, a foot long, and two inches in diameter, which, agitated, become *vividly luminous.*"

Fire-flies are very common in Mexico and South America, and a similar species is found in Africa; they "shine by so strong a *phosphoric* light that a person may read by the light of three of them."

Some of these insects have three luminous patches, one on each side of the head, and one on the under part of the body. The light continues *for some time* after the fly is dead. The light of the *glow-worm* is too well-known to need description. The light is only emitted when they are in motion, and it arises from the two last rings of the abdomen. "Their remains are *phosphorescent.*"

"The great American bittern has the power of emitting a light from its breast equal to the light of a torch."

"*Luminosity* has been noticed chiefly in fungi. A species of agaric, in Western Australia, is said to afford a phosphorescent light of sufficient intensity to read by. Decaying wood, called *touchwood,* caused by the mycelium of fungi, is often phosphorescent; and in Brazil certain mushrooms give out a light like that of fire-flies."

The snail, millepedes, and other insects are distinctly luminous in the dark, as are the mackerel, herring, and many other fish.

Von Humboldt, speaking of the *medusæ* found in sea water, says: "They observed, after it became dark, that none of the three species of medusæ which they had collected emitted light unless they were slightly shaken. When a very irritable individual is placed on a tin plate, and the latter is struck with a piece of metal, the vibrations of the tin are sufficient to make the animal shine. Sometimes, on galvanising medusæ, the phosphorescence appears at the moment when the chain closes, although the exciters are not in direct contact with the body of the subject. The *fingers, after touching it, remain luminous* for two or three minutes. Wood, on being *rubbed* with a medusa, *becomes luminous,* and after the phosphorescence has ceased it may be *rekindled by passing the dry hand over it."* Again, "On their return to the latter of these (Gaurabo), the travellers were much struck by the prodigious number of *phosphorescent* insects which illuminated the grass and foliage. These insects (*elater noctilucus*) are occasionally used for a lamp, being placed in a calabash perforated with holes ; and a young woman at Trinidad informed them that, during a long passage from the mainland, she always had recourse to this *light* when she gave her child the breast at night, the captain not allowing any other on board for fear of pirates."

We have ourselves seen the grass shrubs and underwood of forests brightly illuminated and glittering with *luminous* insects; and the waves of the ocean brilliant with vivid fire from the light emitted by species of medusæ; and, where we have been enabled to procure specimens, we found that in most of them the light was phosphorescent; in many cases, the fingers remained luminous after touching them, and from many we were enabled to obtain luminous solutions of phosphorus.

Now do these numerous *luminous* beings of animated nature, both vegetable and animal, obtain their phosphorus from phosphates ?

As it is our desire to avoid theory or speculation until we have sufficient evidence to say positively "yes" or " no," we will leave the subject of the *source* of the *phosphorus* existing in the brain and other structures of man, by asking the following questions :

1. Does man " by a chemical decomposition, the nature of which it is not easy to explain," extract the phosphorus existing in his system from phosphates contained in the articles of his diet?

2. Does he obtain it partly from phosphates, and partly from elsewhere ?

3. Does he derive it solely from *another* source ?

Whatever the *source* of the phosphorus of the brain may be, it is clear that it must first exist in the blood, and be carried by it to the brain, which we may therefore compare to a *gland,* one purpose of which is for the secretion or absorption of phosphorus from the blood—to collect it and fix it in its own substance, for the purpose of taking part in some of the most important functions and manifestations of the vital phenomena—both perceptible and imperceptible—incidental to, and essentially part of, that as yet incomprehensible and indefinable condition which we term *Life :* the elements or the materials of which it is built we may eventually become thoroughly acquainted with, but the plan will remain obscure—the design is known to the Architect alone.

Direct experiment, and many records on the chemical pathology of the brain, show that although phosphates by their gradual deposition often increase in the brain, the quantity of oxidisable phosphorus *decreases* in "old age."

The foregoing few remarks on phosphorus we have made to show the great importance of this substance in the animal economy—to briefly demonstrate the interesting and instructive properties and manifest influence which it bears towards many of the observed and comprehensible phenomena of organic life, in the hope that many of these phenomena may not long remain questions or problems for futurity to solve; and further to verify the statement which we made in our first chapter, that "this great vital principle, which is centred in the cerebro-spinal axis, gradually wanes, because the brain and nerves by degrees lose their supply of blood, their powers of selection and imbibition, and are deprived of their ordained nourishment, by means of this gradual process of induration and ossification."

We do not state that phosphorus is itself a vital principle, but that it plays an important part in the phenomena of organic life; and as the brain must of necessity derive its supply of phosphorus from the blood, which circulates in vessels which, as we have already shown, gradually indurate, ossify, and become lessened in calibre as age advances, so must the brain and nerves gradually lose their powers of selection and imbibition, and be deprived of their ordained nourishment—and so does the quantity of oxidisable phosphorus in the brain decrease in "old age." Hence the gradual impairment of the functions of the brain and nerves, and the numerous actions dependent, directly or indirectly, upon these delicate and exquisitely formed organs.

The reason that phosphorus, which, as Magendie says, "would seem to have affected almost resurrections," has been so little regarded, is entirely owing to the want of a reliable preparation.

In the present day it is used in the form of "pills" combined with balsam of tolu, yellow wax, and similar vehicles; it is also used dissolved in sulphuric ether, chloroform, rectified alcohol, etc.; and it is also given internally in solution in almond, olive, and codliver oils.

If water is added to the ethereal or alcoholic solutions, the phosphorus precipitates. In the form of pills it is insoluble in water; also insoluble in the blood, and little, if any, of the phosphorus in these preparations is really absorbed into, and assimilated by, the system. Again, owing to the inflammability of phosphorus in the solid form, it may produce inflammation and even ulceration of the stomach and bowels; we may therefore unhesitatingly say, that any form of phosphorus where *solid particles* are either present or are produced by the addition of water, is, to say the least, unreliable and uncertain in its action, and may be dangerous in its use. Even in solution in oil, we have on one occasion seen sufficient irritation produced to result in a disease analogous in appearance and characters to erysipelas.*

---

* This may be due to the particles of oil holding phosphorus in solution, and incapable of further subdivision, being arrested in the capillaries supplying the skin.

It is therefore only just and correct to state that the preparations of phosphorus generally used are not satisfactory in their results.

Thick syrup, mucilage, and several similar compounds have the property of retaining free phosphorus —not in mechanical, but in aqueous solution—if transmitted to them by means of a proper medium or volatile solvent.   As an instance, if we dissolve in sulphuric ether as much phosphorus as the ether will take up, and add, we will say, from thirty to sixty drops of this solution to a pint of thick syrup, shake them together, allow the ether to evaporate, and decant the greater portion of the syrup, leaving a small quantity at the bottom of the vessel, which retains what solid particles of phosphorus may have precipitated, the upper or decanted part is perfectly clear and transparent, and will be found to contain in aqueous—not in mechanical— solution sufficient phosphorus, even in doses of one or two drachms, to distinctly influence and increase the amount of phosphates in the liquid excretions.

By using glycerine instead of the syrup, we may obtain even a stronger preparation than the above. Here we have two preparations of phosphorus in aqueous solution, and although they contain but a small proportion, it is in a form which cannot precipitate, and which may be readily absorbed into the system.   Small doses only are required, for the whole is assimilated, whereas in most of the preparations in which a thirty-sixth or even a twentieth part of a grain per dose are given, only a fraction serves its desired use, and the remaining portion is often passed out of the system unchanged.

In the present age of rapidity and despatch, phosphorus is often a deficient constituent of the brain and nerves. It is often wasted in the turmoil of business, in anxious moments pending loss or success, in grief and sadness, and the acute trials arising from family and other bereavements; in the mental applications and exertions of the scholar, to whatever section of science he may be attached; in even the excessive indulgences and libations of the inebriate, who delights in the stimulant and unconsciously in the solvent properties of alcohol—which in excess dissolves and removes phosphorus from his brain—hence the tremor and other symptoms dependent upon a deficiency of nerve power.

To demonstrate the action of phosphorus upon the system, after its absorption into the blood, we may divide it into two portions. One part is carried by the circulation to the brain, which assimilates and fixes it in its own substance; thus serving to take part in— even to increase—many of the mental and nervous phenomena of organic life. The other part is carried by the general circulation to every structure and organ of the body. During its passage it fixes and combines with oxygen existing in the blood, and becomes hypophosphorous, afterwards phosphoric acid. Phosphorus therefore combines with oxygen existing in the blood, and by this means *prevents excessive oxidation* or waste of the system; again, when on its union with oxygen it becomes phosphoric acid, it combines with the alkaline and *earthy* bases existing in the blood, forming neutral salts; and further, as the amount of phosphoric acid increases, part of the insoluble earthy compounds (which have been gradually deposited) become super-phosphates, which are soluble—which circulate again in the blood, and part of which are *removed from the system* in the liquid excretions—thus *preventing the accumulation of earthy compounds* in the system, and even *removing those which have* been already *deposited.*

Phosphorus, therefore, by its great affinity for oxygen, prevents the undue accumulation of fibrinous and gelatinous substances in the system, and on its becoming phosphoric acid, removes the earthy matter which has gradually accumulated—which we have termed "ossification"—which is the chief *cause* of "old age," and "natural death ;" thereby, in the full sense of the term, *prolonging life for a lengthened period !* *Hypophosphites* have a similar action, they fix oxygen from the blood, and *become phosphates,* thus preventing undue waste of the system.

This is the reason—and the only one—that the hypophosphites act so beneficially in consumption.* The *alkaline* hypophosphites only are of service for the purpose now under consideration.

° As two of perhaps the latest views on consumption, it is stated that consumption is due to a *lack of oxidisable phosphorus* in the system ; again, that it is caused by *mineral inanition.* Now both these are *characteristics* of the disease. Atmospheric oxygen oxidises phosphorus excessively in consumption, there is therefore a lack of oxidisable phosphorus in the body. This again gives rise to an excess of phosphoric acid, which removes alkaline and earthy salts from the system ; we have therefore so-called "defective mineral nutrition." But neither of these are *causes,* they are but the results—*effects*—of a distinct and demonstrable cause, as is also the formation of tubercle.—*Vide* "Consumption, a Re-investigation of its Cause," by the Author.

11

Phosphoric acid possesses but the one action, that of preventing undue accumulation, and of removing earthy compounds from the system, which action we have already considered.   Therefore in the agents best adapted to prolong life for a *lengthened period,* we notice chiefly distilled water used daily as a drink ; unoxidised phosphorus, in syrup, glycerine, etc., in doses of one or two drachms, according to the strength of the solution ; the *alkaline* hypophosphites, and the dilute phosphoric acid (corresponding to ten per cent. by weight of the anhydrous acid) in doses of from ten to twenty drops, well diluted with water.   These preparations may be taken two or three times daily (according to the *degree* of ossification), as an article of *diet,* and not as a *medicine.*

It would naturally be asked that, if life were pro-longed by means of the diet and the agents herein mentioned, what state of body would be the con-comitant of such existence ? To this we answer, that the *cause* being to a great extent *suspended,* the effect could not follow so quickly and prematurely as it otherwise would.   For the many organs and structures could not so readily harden and ossify.   The numerous charac-teristics of "old age" could not exist to the same extent ; and a state of mental and bodily juvenescence would be maintained for a lengthened period.

CHAPTER VI.

CONCLUSION.

SCIENCE dictates, and even the most casual observer, who—for purpose or principle—attempts to comprehend the truths and phenomena of universal Nature, unhesitatingly admits that " every *phenomenon* has its *reason,* every *effect* its *cause.*" This is a fact established and indisputable; but how often are the *laws of life* and *of death* doomed to be overlooked by the deluded, and even removed from their legitimate situation, which they of necessity embrace in forming volumes in the library of the academy of Nature ! For the sake of method, we classify and arrange under many heads, which are but servitors to avoid a chaos of observations, descriptions and deductions ; the confusions thus avoided obviously present themselves, but one branch of science is dependent upon another—each forms a part, all united a whole—for Nature is one. To recognise one and ignore another portion of an entirety— each part of which is dependent upon unity—is to break a rule which remains unbroken. To say that everything dies simply because it has lived—that the age of man is *fixed* irrespective of reason or cause—is not only presumption, but confessedly a want of conception, a disbelief in what is and therefore must be, and an assault on the fixed and immutable laws of natural phenomena.

When we reflect or meditate on the progress of civilised man, we notice wonders and improvements in his surroundings, for his welfare and comfort; we discover

a spirit of inquiry amongst men, a silent march of
thought—a steady progress, impelled forward by an
eternal law—Nature's law—experience. This law we
may compare to a circle; the beginning we know not,
the end we know not. This circle enlarges, expands—
where is the limit ? Opposition, reproach, threats and
violence can only be a temporary check; they cannot
control, abate or arrest the progress of inquiry, the
keenness of research, the results of experience. But
amongst the varied and expanding objects of research,
is not that inquiry which appertains to the preservation
of life the most important of all to humanity ?

What is man without health, even if endowed with
riches ! Take away the latter and their accompany-
ing luxuries—only give him health; this accomplished,
the first desire is a return of the riches. But with
both a word remains which we hate to utter, a thought
we dread to contemplate, a thing which gives sorrow,
pain and grief. That word, that thought, that thing
is *Death*. Even in cases where life appears a burden,
how tenaciously do men cling to it ! How the spirit
recoils from a struggle with Death ! How fondly it
retains its grasp of life ! Man's great desire is for
health and long life on earth, but to this there are
some few exceptions—the result of incidental impressions. "Man clings to the world as his home, and
would fain live here for ever."

"And can we see the newly-turned earth of so
many graves, hear the almost hourly-sounding knell
that announces the departure of another soul from its
bodily fabric, meet our associates clad in the garb of
woe, hear of death after death among those whom we

knew—perhaps respected, perhaps loved—without pausing to consider if we may not seek and haply find *more than the mere causes,* find the *means of checking* the premature dissolution that so painfully excites the deepest and most hidden sympathies of our nature ?"

"*The prolongation of the life* of the people must become an essential part of family, municipal and national policy. Although it is right and glorious to incur risks and to sacrifice life for public objects, it has always been felt that length of days is the measure, and that the completion by the people of the full term of natural existence is the groundwork of their felicity. For untimely death is a great evil. What is so bitter as the premature death of a wife, a child, a father ? What dashes to the earth so many hopes, breaks so many auspicious enterprises, as the unnatural death ? The poets, as faithful interpreters of our aspirations, have always sung, that *in the happier ages of the world this source of tears shall be dried up.*"—Registrar-General of England.

In the present day, when we are so accustomed to wonders that they no longer excite our wonder; when we send our thoughts almost round the world with the velocity of lightning; when we hear voices miles away by the agency of the telephone; the tick of a watch—even the tramp of a fly—by the microphone; when we transcribe the vibrations of sound with the precision of a mathematician; when we freeze water into ice in white-hot crucibles; when we cast copper into statues without the aid of heat; when it is possible to illuminate cities without gas—with lamps devoid of flame or fire; when some of the most precious minerals are produced from their elements; when we believe that to-morrow even the diamond may be artificially produced; with all these wonders recently brought to light for the benefit of mankind, is man *himself* to be debarred from that social progress which is daily manifested ? Are the achievements of science of no avail in benefiting his degenerated existence ? Will not our daily-increasing knowledge of nature and the behaviour of her elements eventually tend to this end ? In reference to which Liebig asks : "Is that knowledge not the *philosopher's stone*, which promises to disclose to us the laws of life, and which *must finally yield to us the means of curing diseases and of prolonging life ?*"

The fields of research become richer and wider with every new discovery, which is often as precious, if not more useful than gold—actually a transmutation for the benefit and comfort of man. But as yet he has *himself* been little benefited by science, which must of necessity ultimately dictate a *means* of curing diseases and of prolonging life. Is it even just, in the present day of so-called wisdom, to ridicule the alchemists of old, who diligently laboured and searched for a "virgin earth"—a mysterious substance which would " change the baser metals to gold, and be a means of curing diseases, of restoring youth to the exhausted frame of age, and of prolonging life indefinitely" ? Such a view would be utterly unjust. For the present science of chemistry owes its position, its existence—perhaps its origin—to the untiring observations and researches of the alchemists, which were instilled into them in their laborious searches for the " philosopher's stone."

All they sought for exists, and may ultimately be found in the illimitable science of chemistry.

Oxygen it is that by combining with the substance of fuel during combustion, causes the consumption of that fuel. Oxygen it is that by combining in a similar manner with the substance of the human body, chiefly during respiration, causes the waste of the system and the necessity for food. Oxygen it is that corrodes and eats away the solid masonry of palaces, castles, mansions and churches, and eventually crumbles them to dust. Iron bridges, marble monuments, massive structures—of whatever architecture or material—must eventually succumb to this all-destroying agent.

The Roman proverb runs, " *Tempus edax rerum,*" Time, the consumer of all things. But Time would be of no avail without oxygen, which is really the " *edax rerum.*"

Time is also credited with the changes which take place in the human body between youth and old age; but oxygen it is which, by wasting man's tissues, necessitates his supplying himself with food, which food contains earthy and obstructive matter, which matter by accumulating in the numerous organs and structures, increases his density and rigidity, and by hardening the same produces the various characteristics, both in appearance and texture, of old age, and by stiffening his joints, that decrepitude and inactivity which, in conjunction with the induration and ossification of the numerous organs, causes the human machine gradually to move slower and slower, and ultimately to stop, and die a " natural death."

Thus it is seen that oxygen, though necessary to

support life, is the primary cause, by necessitating food, of those changes which are only so many steps from the cradle to the grave. The paradox therefore exists, that even while we breathe the breath of life, we also inhale the *" edax rerum"* which only requires *Time* to bring about our destruction.

We may therefore say that *oxygen* is but the *primary cause*, because it necessitates food; and that the *earthy* and obstructive *matter* contained in that food is the immediate and *actual cause*, inasmuch as it gradually gives rise to rigidity, ossification and death.

As a jet kept free from clogging and obstructive matter, and supplied with pure gas, will continue to burn, independent of time, so the human body, supplied with food free from earthy and obstructive matter, will retain the flame of life.

The beneficial effects of fruit as an article of diet, both in health and disease, cannot be over-rated. In health the apple, the pear, the grape, the strawberry, the gooseberry, the tomato, the fig, the date, wall-fruits, the melon, and numerous others, present such a field for choice that the most capricious appetite need never be disappointed. The supply of fruit in the United Kingdom is not great, but considerable quantities of both fresh and preserved fruits are imported from all parts of the world, and are rapidly becoming popular amongst all classes; and it is to be hoped that our fellow-countrymen will gradually become more alive to the benefits to be derived from a more general and frequent use of fruits as an article of daily food.

" When pain and anguish wring the brow," in slight and temporary indispositions, or during prolonged febrile diseases, what is more refreshing and beneficial than the juice of the luscious orange ? Indeed, in many parts of the world, especially in tropical regions, the juice of the orange taken in large quantities has been found to be a specific for many descriptions of fever ; it is in fact Nature's remedy, and an unsurpassed one.

Cereal and farinaceous foods form the basis of the diet of so-called " vegetarians," who are not guided by any *direct* principle, except that they believe it is wrong to eat animal food.   For this reason vegetarians enjoy no better health, and live no longer than those around them.   Our remarks, therefore, apply to fruits as distinct from vegetables.

We have shown a means of partially arresting the never-ceasing action of atmospheric oxygen ; less food, therefore, would be necessary to support life.   We have also demonstrated a means of supplying a substance which gradually becomes deficient as age advances, which deficiency is only due to the immediate and *actual* cause of old age—the accumulation of earthy matter in the system, which may also be prevented, and even removed, when already deposited.   All these actions are combined in the one substance—*free phosphorus*.

The earthy matter may be also removed by hypophosphorous acid, by phosphoric acid, and by the daily use of *distilled* water as a drink.   By these means we can therefore prolong life in the full sense of the term, for a *lengthened* period.

It has been said that " men are more often governed by words and phrases than by facts and realities ;"*

* Lord Beaconsfield.

this is not always the case, but did a man require visible proof that another of the same age could prolong his life even to a hundred years, by the means *herein mentioned*, that sceptic would have to devise another means of prolonging his own life to enable him to see the completion of that term of years by the other.

Of all our divisions of science, perhaps the most important of all to humanity is medicine, and as one branch of science is dependent upon another, so is medicine dependent upon physiological chemistry, and has to patiently await its advance. Medicine, as yet far from complete, is a collection of the labours of ages, and has for its own particular purpose a view to the good of mankind.

In our numerous searches for a definition of the treatment of disease, we find none so simple, clear, and may be correct as that given seventeen hundred years ago by Galen, a physician of Pergamus, which is to supply that which is deficient by communication, and to remove that which is in excess by means of a remedy which tends to abstract it. This is a perfect definition for the removal of disease, and for the restoration of health; and when physiological chemistry is sufficiently advanced to tell us undoubtedly which elements are deficient, and which are in excess, and when we are further able to supply or remove them, then will medicine be perfect—then will it take its place as the first, foremost, and most indispensable science—the most important of all to humanity.

In relation to the bodily state of "old age," and the possibility of delaying such a state of the system,

Galen's definition has been irresistibly forced upon us. For we find in old age that earthy and other solid matter is in excess, and that phosphorus is to a certain extent deficient. The remedy is to remove that which is in excess, and to restore that which is deficient.

In an oration delivered before the Medical Society of London, Dr. B. W. Richardson said: "I think I am not far wrong in making the general confession, that out of all our collection of details, gathered from time immemorial, we have never as yet eliminated so much as one great and fundamental law relating to diseases as a whole."

This deficiency in the first place arises to a great extent from a general acceptance of hypotheses as explanations of phenomena. What is "discovered" to-day is so likely to be contradicted to-morrow, "for the truth lies in the statement that in medicine *experiment,* as a rule, is turned into *hypothesis,* and not into *fact.*" This is the great cause of its comparatively slow progress, and wherever hypothesis is erroneous, more patience and a longer period are required to prove it to be so, than the time occupied in its construction. In the second place, this deficiency arises from the tardy development of physiological chemistry. Let us, however, not decry medicine for these reasons, let us rather strive to advance it. For, as Sir Thomas Watson so justly observes: "The profession of medicine, having for its end the common good of mankind, knows nothing of national enmities, of political strife, of sectarian divisions. Disease and pain the sole conditions of its ministry, it is disquieted by no misgivings concerning the justice or honour of its clients' caused ;

but dispenses its peculiar benefits without stint or scruple, to men of every country and party and rank and religion, and to men of no religion at all."

In considering exclusively the subject before us, does not the action of atmospheric oxygen upon the system—especially when excessive—and also the gradual accumulation of earthy and other solid matter in the body, with its numerous and abstruse divergencies, open out to us a world of new ideas in regard to the fundamental causes of many diseases ?

In conclusion, we may say, that, although the desire for long life exists as a natural, prevalent, and deeply-rooted love, there are, through continued trial and disappointment, many exceptions ; in fact the present subject is not acceptable to all. Our remarks are therefore confined to those who believe that, " In this world there is, or might be, more sunshine than rain, more joy than sorrow, more love than hate, more smiles than tears. The good heart, the tender feeling, and the pleasant disposition make smiles, love, and sunshine everywhere."

In the pages of Nature are distinctly and legibly written—to those who will refer but with patience— the laws of life and the laws of death ; and in clear, unmistakable characters the reason—the cause—of the *ultimate* death of every animate being. There are abundant materials for investigation and research ; the cause of " old age " in man is demonstrated, and a means of checking it has herein been clearly explained ; and it would not be contrary to the dictates of our nature to hope that *science* may be incited into an inquiry for more general perfection, which may be the means of actually conquering it :

> " By showing conclusively and clearly,
> That Death is a stupid blunder merely,
> And not a necessity of our lives."
>
> LONGFELLOW.

APPENDIX.

Owing to the general objection to Biblical quotations being given as part of a scientific subject, we *append* the following Canonical and Apocryphal extracts, not for the purpose of proving, or necessarily to verify, but to show their coincidence with what we have demonstrated to be possible on scientific grounds :

" God created man *to be immortal*, and made him to be an image of His own eternity."

" And the Lord God commanded the man, saying, Of every tree of the garden thou *mayest* freely eat ;* but of the tree of the knowledge of good and evil, thou shalt not eat of it; for in the day that thou eatest thereof *thou shalt surely die.*"

" And the woman said unto the serpent, We may eat of the *fruit of the trees* of the garden; but of the tree which is in the midst of the garden, God hath said, Ye shall not eat of it, neither shall ye touch it, *lest ye die.*"

" And unto Adam He said, Because thou hast hearkened unto the voice of thy wife, and hast eaten of the

* Hebrew : " *Eating, thou shalt eat.*"

tree, of which I commanded thee, saying, Thou shalt *not* eat of it; cursed is the *ground* for thy sake; in sorrow shalt thou *eat of it* all the days of thy life."

" And the Lord God said, Behold, the man is become as one of us, to know good and evil; and now, LEST *he* put forth his hand, and *take also of the tree of life*, and eat, and LIVE FOR EVER: therefore the Lord God sent him forth from the garden of Eden, to till the ground from whence he was taken."

" For God made not death : *neither hath He pleasure* in the destruction of the living."

" For He created all things that they might have their being : and the generations of the world *were* healthful : and there is no poison of destruction in them, nor the *kingdom of death* upon the earth."

" But ungoldly men with their works and words called it to them."

" And (our fathers) received the *laws of life*, which they kept not."

" Know this therefore, that they which are left behind are more blessed than they that be dead."

" If therefore thou shalt destroy him, which with so great labour was fashioned, it is an easy thing to be ordained by thy commandment, that the thing which was made might be *preserved*."

" Oh, thou Adam ! what hast thou done ? for though it was thou that sinned, thou art not fallen alone, but we that come of thee."

" For what profit is it unto us if there be promised an immortal time, whereas we have done the works that bring death ?"

" For they shall also pray unto the Lord, that He

would prosper that which they give for ease, and *remedy to prolong life."*

" Behold I show you a mystery; *we shall not all sleep*, but we shall all be changed . . . . then shall be brought to pass the saying that is written, Death is swallowed up in victory."

" The face of the covering cast over all people, and the veil that is spread over all nations shall be destroyed, and *death swallowed up in victory."*

" I have no pleasure in the death of him that dieth, saith the Lord God, wherefore *turn yourselves and live ye."*

Members of many religious denominations believe that there will be a day when " they shall sit every man under his *vine* and under his *fig-tree*, and none shall make them afraid."

" In that day, saith the Lord of Hosts, shall ye call every man his neighbour under the *vine* and under the *fig-tree."*

" And they shall beat their swords into ploughshares and their spears into *pruning-hooks."*

" And they shall plant *vineyards*, and *eat the fruit of them."*

" There shall be no more thence an infant of days, nor an old man that hath not filled his days : for the *child* shall die an *hundred* years old."

" Behold the days come, saith the Lord, that the ploughman shall *overtake* the reaper, and *the treader of grapes him that soweth seed* . . . . and they shall plant *vineyards*, and drink the wine thereof; they shall also *make gardens, and eat the fruit of them."*

" And there shall be no more death ; neither sorrow, nor crying, neither shall there be any more pain."

" The last enemy that shall be destroyed is death."

That which is true is true absolutely ; materially and spiritually. It cannot therefore be claimed that this language of Scripture has exclusively a spiritual reference. Whatever the objections to these quotations may be (if any), we may observe that many are led away into atheistic and materialistic views, against their own will, contrary to the very yearnings of their inner nature, by the dictates of science ; they are pulled forcibly away, they are dragged by a chain composed of links, each one of which is a theory of the day, and which we may again compare to the metals. Of these links some few are golden, true, lasting and eternal; others are but as the baser metals—oxidisable, destructible. Those which are erroneous must corrode and decay—be destroyed by the advances of investigation; they must become, as it were, but as oxides of the earths, trampled upon, unnoticed, forgotten, and eventually wrapt in the cloak of oblivion.

THE END.

LONDON : BAILLIÈRE, TINDALL, AND COX, 20, KING WILLIAM STREET.

www.ingramcontent.com/pod-product-compliance
Lightning Source LLC
Chambersburg PA
CBHW031110020726
47495CB00007B/2131